D0257187

POPPY

IN THE

FIELD

Also by Mary Hooper

Historical fiction

At the Sign of the Sugared Plum
Petals in the Ashes
The Fever and the Flame
(a special omnibus edition of the two books above)
The Remarkable Life and Times of Eliza Rose
At the House of the Magician
By Royal Command
The Betrayal
Fallen Grace
Velvet
The Disgrace of Kitty Grey

Contemporary fiction

Megan
Megan 2
Megan 3
Holly
Amy
Two Sides of the Story
Zara
Poppy

POPPY IN THE FIELD

MARY HOOPER

BLOOMSBURY

LONDON NEW DELHI NEW YORK SYDNEY

Bloomsbury Publishing, London, New Delhi, New York and Sydney

First published in Great Britain in May 2015 by Bloomsbury Publishing Plc
50 Bedford Square, London WC1B 3DP

www.bloomsbury.com

Bloomsbury is a registered trademark of Bloomsbury Publishing Plc

Copyright © Mary Hooper 2015

The moral right of the author has been asserted

All rights reserved
No part of this publication may be reproduced or
transmitted by any means, electronic, mechanical, photocopying
or otherwise, without the prior permission of the publisher

A CIP catalogue record for this book is available from the British Library

ISBN 978 1 4088 2763 5

Typeset by Integra Software Services Pvt. Ltd.
Printed and bound in Great Britain by CPI Group (UK) Ltd, Croydon CR0 4YY

1 3 5 7 9 10 8 6 4 2

www.bloomsbury.com
www.maryhooper.co.uk

For Molly

Chapter One

'Pearson!'

Poppy, freezing cold, miserable and intent on getting to bed, heard her name called and paused on the stairs. Turning, she saw that her friend Essie Matthews had just come through the swing doors of the nurses' hostel.

Matthews ran up the stairs towards her. 'So how was your Christmas Day?' she asked, pink-cheeked and puffing after a brisk walk from the station. 'Did the boys in your ward love their Christmas stockings? Did you have a good time?'

Poppy, with some effort, just about managed to smile. *Good*, she thought, wasn't quite the word for it.

Catching up with her, Matthews linked arms. 'Did Father Christmas bring you any surprises?'

'Nothing special,' Poppy said. There would be time enough the next day to tell Matthews about the surprise – the rather terrible surprise – she'd had. She didn't want to talk about it right then, though. She wanted to get into bed, pull the blanket over her head and sleep until the new year. 'What about you?' she asked. 'I expect your ma was really pleased to see you.'

'She was – but, to be honest, it was all a bit bleak at home. My sister couldn't get leave from her hospital and my brother's train from Lancashire was cancelled at the last moment, so it was just Ma and me.' She looked at Poppy enquiringly. 'But what was it like at Netley? I missed being there, you know. Did your boys enjoy themselves?'

Poppy nodded. 'They did.' She and Matthews were VADs, members of the Voluntary Aid Detachment affiliated to the Red Cross. One of Poppy's nicest duties as a volunteer nurse had been to make sure all the men in her ward had Christmas stockings and presents. 'They squabbled over the toy cars as if they were five-year-olds,' she said, 'but, you know, just the fact that they're back in Blighty is enough to keep them happy.'

Matthews nodded, understanding at once what she meant, for Netley Hut Hospital in Southampton, where Poppy and Matthews worked, was the main receiving hospital for casualties from France and Belgium. Every Tommy there, however badly injured in the war, was happy to be back in England to have his wounds treated.

'But you look a bit . . . peaky, if you don't mind me saying,' Matthews said, looking at her curiously. 'Did anything else happen? Did you get a convoy of injured men in or something?'

2

'Not a bit of it!' Poppy said, falsely bright. 'We lit the Christmas lanterns, the boys smoked their Christmas cigarettes, ate their chocolate and wrote letters on their new notepaper.' She paused and added, 'At least, those who had use of their arms wrote letters. I wrote two or three for them, and then . . .' her eyes suddenly filled with tears and she couldn't help but blurt out, 'then I wrote a letter of my own!'

'What d'you mean?' Matthews asked. 'Did one of the boys die today?' Both girls, trained in the basics of nursing, had witnessed tragedy: patients they had thought were ready to go home having unexpected complications and dying suddenly. When this happened, the ward sister or one of the nurses would write straight away to the man's next of kin.

Poppy shook her head. 'No, it wasn't that. I'd best wait and tell you about it tomorrow.'

'Gosh, you've got me really intrigued now.'

'It's not anything to do with a patient – and it's little enough compared to what any of them have gone through, but . . .' She brushed a tear from her cheek. 'Oh, I wasn't going to say anything. Not tonight.'

Matthews looked at her, concerned. 'Tell me now or you'll never get to sleep,' she said.

Knowing this was true, Poppy allowed herself to be led back down the stairs and into the deserted hostel canteen.

The building had once been a Young Women's Christian Association centre, but had been taken over entirely by the Red Cross for its VADs, most of whom were working at the same hospital as Poppy. Usually the canteen was smoky and busy, the pungent aroma of frying bacon in the air, but that evening the big square room was bare and cold and all the chairs were up on the tables. This was because most of the girls had decided to go home for Christmas, or stay at the hospital and have their meals with the patients. There were a few paper chains trailed about, and a rather forlorn-looking fir tree, but apart from these, little to indicate it was Christmas. There was a war on, of course, and any seasonal extras had gone to the front line in the hopes of making the men's lives in the trenches – and being away from their loved ones – a little more bearable.

Matthews got down two chairs from the nearest table and gently pushed her friend into one. 'Tell me every-thing,' she said, sitting down in the other. 'I know something rotten must have happened by the look on your face. You're as white as a bleached sheet.'

A moment went by, then a tear rolled down Poppy's cheek and splashed on to the tin table. 'It's Freddie,' she said, meaning Freddie de Vere, the handsome, rather dashing son of the family she used to work for as a parlourmaid.

'Not . . . not dead?' Matthews asked in horror, for Freddie had recently taken a commission in the army and his regiment had been fighting in France, close to the front line.

Poppy shook her head. 'Not that.'

Matthews stared at her. 'Is he injured . . . disabled . . . blinded?'

'No,' Poppy said. 'None of those.' She heaved a sigh. 'I know it's pathetic of me to be such a drip what with everything else that's going on, but I found out that he's become engaged. He's due to get married while he's on his Christmas leave.'

Matthews stared at her, looking outraged. 'Married? Never! He's been leading you on for months, then!'

'I know.' Poppy's head drooped. She and Freddie had exchanged several letters, he'd taken her for afternoon tea in Southampton, and from the things he'd said, she'd rather allowed herself to think that there was a future in their relationship.

'Who on earth is he marrying?'

'The lovely Miss Philippa Cardew,' Poppy said bitterly, picturing the girl in question: Freddie's childhood sweetheart, all Parisian fashion, elfin face and glossy bobbed hair. As a parlourmaid, Poppy had seen (and served tea to) Miss Cardew on several occasions when she'd been working at Airey House, the ancestral home of the de Veres.

'What a beast!' Matthews said fiercely. 'How could he do that? How could he treat you so?'

'Quite easily, it seems.'

'But however did you find out?'

'It was in one of Jameson's society magazines,' Poppy said. 'There was a photograph of Miss Cardew and a few lines saying that she and Second Lieutenant Frederick de Vere had become engaged and would marry quietly during the Christmas period.' She sighed. 'I know it's pathetic of me but I keep picturing her in white velvet with an ermine stole, looking very beautiful.'

Matthews smiled sympathetically and patted her hand.

'I expect they're getting the de Vere family jewels out of store for the occasion,' Poppy said.

'Oh, what a rotten thing for him to do – after allowing you to think he cared for you. I've a good mind to go and disrupt the wedding!'

'I thought about doing that, too,' Poppy said, managing to smile. 'I could run down the aisle of the chapel and stop the show.'

'Write to his commanding officer.'

'Or his mother!' Poppy said, thinking about the letter she'd received several months ago from Freddie's mother, warning her not to see Freddie again. A mere parlourmaid was never going to be good enough for her darling boy.

'I'd do better than that,' Matthews said. 'I'd turn up at the wedding with a cushion stuffed up my frock and say I was in the family way!'

Poppy began laughing, which led in turn to tears and then, after a while, to her feeling a little less desperate. She dried her cheeks, took off her nurse's cap and blew her nose on a clean handkerchief. 'But there's something else to tell you.'

'One shock at a time, please.'

'I told you that I wrote a letter . . .'

'You wrote to him. Good! I hope you jolly well told him what an utter cad he is! I hope you –'

'It wasn't a letter to Freddie,' Poppy interrupted. 'It was . . . Well, this afternoon, after I realised I'd lost Freddie, I had a good long think about things and I decided I wanted to do something more.'

'For the war?'

Poppy nodded. 'So I spoke to Sister about it and then wrote to the Recruitment Office at Devonshire House, requesting a posting abroad.'

Matthews looked at her with something between admiration and horror. 'Not really?!'

'I want to get right into the middle of it. I want to go to France or Belgium.'

'Are you sure? It's horrifically dangerous. My sister told me that it's much worse out there than anyone's saying.'

Poppy shrugged. 'I know.'

'You're not going just because of him, are you? Because you're thinking that life's not worth living or some such rot?'

'Of course not!' she protested. 'I thought a while back that I'd like to be closer to the action – perhaps look after the troops straight off the front line – but I didn't apply because I thought that staying here in Southampton would make it easier to see Freddie whenever he came through. And now . . . well, that's obviously not going to happen, is it, so why should I stay? What is there to keep me here? And they're really desperate for more nurses out there.'

'I know, but personally I don't know if I'd be up to it. I mean, the injuries, the blood and gore . . .'

'My friend at Netley – you know, the doctor?'

'Michael Archer,' Matthews said, naming the newly qualified young doctor who'd struck up a friendship with Poppy.

'Yes, him. He said that medics have realised that the sooner a casualty is attended to – examined, operated on, rested and cared for – the better his chances of pulling through.'

Matthews nodded sombrely. 'The golden hour, they call it. It sounds sensible.'

'I'd really like to be part of that.'

'But I thought you have to be older than we are to nurse in Flanders?'

'You're supposed to be, but the truth is, they're so desperate for competent nurses that they hardly ask now. The main thing is that you've proved you're a good worker. Sister Kay put the idea in my head – she's leaving Netley for a casualty clearing station and she's promised to sponsor me.'

'Oh.' For a moment, Matthews looked forlorn. 'I shall miss you awfully.'

'You won't have time to miss me! We're all going to be horrendously busy. 1916 is going to be the year of the Big Push, isn't it? When the outcome of the war gets decided.'

'So they say,' said Matthews.

'Why don't you come with me?'

'Hmm,' Matthews said. 'I'll think about it.' She looked at Poppy closely. 'I'm not trying to make you feel worse, but you look done in. Why don't we get our hot-water bottles filled and then go to bed. We can plot revenge against Freddie de Vere in the morning.'

Poppy yawned. 'I don't care about a hot-water bottle,' she said. 'I just want to get between those sheets and close my eyes . . .'

The girls had got halfway up the stairs when they heard a screech of brakes in the roadway outside. A moment after that, the swing doors were given a shove so hard that they slammed into the walls on each side, and a khaki-clad soldier ran in. Matthews and Poppy stared at him in alarm.

'Beg yer pardon,' he called, spotting them on the stairs, 'but are you Netley VADs?'

'We are,' Matthews said.

'But it must be nearly eleven o'clock,' Poppy said. 'What is it, an invasion?'

'Sorry about that, but there's an emergency.'

'There must be! What sort of –'

'We've got a convoy coming into the hospital,' he panted. 'Forty or fifty badly injured men, I've been told. Anyone not on leave is requested to get back to Netley as soon as possible.'

'On Christmas night!?' said Matthews. 'Don't the Germans have Christmas?'

'I don't suppose it was Christmas when they were injured,' Poppy said. She yawned again and then shrugged. Her bed was calling to her, but her bed would just have to wait – fifty injured Tommies couldn't.

'I'll run upstairs and wake whoever's around,' Matthews said. 'Though I don't suppose I'll be terribly popular.'

Poppy straightened her nurse's cap and retied the strings under her hair at the back of her neck. She forced a smile at the young soldier. 'Would you be able to give us a lift back to Netley?'

'Of course,' he said. He gave an elaborate bow. 'Especially if all the girls are like you two.'

But Poppy, nursing her broken heart, wasn't in the mood for flirting.

In Hut 59, Sister Kay, still on duty despite the hour, had been doing what she called 'playing shops': shuffling beds containing sleeping patients around the ward to fit in the newcomers, wheeling bedsteads into other wards – even temporarily moving them into the spacious corridors of the main hospital building. Fresh bedding had been brought in, ten new beds for the men who were coming to Ward 59 had been made up, and the ward glowed in the light from the red paper lanterns that the boys had made for Christmas. Poppy knew that for those coming in, after the terrors of the front line and a difficult and pain-filled journey across the Channel, the ward would look like heaven.

The little chiming clock on Sister Kay's desk struck midnight. Sister herself was at the desk doing paper-work, the night staff had gone to find something to eat and Nurse Gallagher had gone to see if she could conjure up an urn of hot water to make cocoa for the new boys when they arrived. The other VAD on the ward, Moffat, was staring out of the window looking for the first signs of them. The nurses had already worked a full day and were quietly willing the casualties to come soon so that they could put them to bed and then take some rest themselves. Poppy hoped that there wouldn't be any who were near death – it would be too awful to inform a family that their son had died on Christmas Day.

She glanced around the ward, looking for a task to keep her occupied, but the ward was perfectly still, perfectly tidy. The only sound was from the men, some of whom were snoring, groaning or coughing in their sleep. It was much too early to start laying up the trays for breakfast, but Poppy, for want of a job, went into the little kitchen and began doing them anyway.

'Salt, pepper, sugar, butter, marmalade, spoon, knife . . .' she murmured to herself, doling them out while trying to stop yawning.

Such a routine job didn't stop her from thinking about Freddie de Vere. About the kisses they'd shared (not exactly passionate, she had to admit – there had never been time for that), the things he'd said. The way he'd always looked at her so intently that, when he'd taken her out to tea, she hadn't been able to eat more than a mouse's portion of anything – all she'd wanted to do was gaze at him. She especially remembered what he'd written in reply to her plea to know where she stood with him; the words he'd used to assure her that Philippa Cardew was nothing more than a childhood friend his mother was very fond of. *I have no intention of marrying Miss Cardew*, he'd said.

'*No intention . . .*' she murmured. Leaning against the little sink in the kitchen, her eyelids fluttered shut and she felt herself swaying.

'Gosh, I've heard the expression "asleep on your feet . . ."' a voice said.

Poppy jumped, suddenly alert, and turned to see Michael Archer standing in the doorway with his arms outstretched.

'I thought I was going to have to catch you!'

'Sorry,' Poppy said. How unprofessional! 'The only excuse I have is that it's well past my bedtime.'

'Just think – if I'd caught you, Sister Kay would probably have come in and discovered us in a compromising position, and we'd both have been disciplined.' His silver-grey eyes flickered and caught hers. 'And I don't suppose your chap would have been very pleased about it, either.'

Poppy, not commenting on any of this banter, turned on the tap in the sink and splashed her face with cold water. 'There! I'm wide awake now,' she said. 'It won't happen again, Doctor Archer.'

'Michael,' he corrected her – as he usually did.

As usual, she pretended not to hear him. Sister Kay was easy-going, kind and fair, but she'd be down like a ton of bricks on a nurse who had the temerity to call a doctor by his first name.

'But why are you still here?' he asked.

'We got a call to come back to the hospital – a convoy's expected.'

'*Was* expected,' he said. 'We've just heard that owing to weather conditions the ship's dropped anchor further down the coast at Dover.'

'Oh! But the beds are ready.'

'I dare say they'll be filled tomorrow – I've heard there are two more hospital ships ready to set off from Calais. Look, I'll go in and tell Sister Kay the latest. She'll confirm it with the commander, then you can go home to bed.'

'That's really decent of you,' Poppy said. 'By the way,' she added as he turned to go, 'I've applied for VAD work in France.'

He raised his eyebrows. 'Good for you. I suppose that's because I'm going to be out there?'

Poppy felt herself blushing. 'Certainly not, Doctor Archer.'

'Michael,' he said.

But Poppy, already reaching for her outdoor coat and anticipating her bed, didn't hear him.

Chapter Two

Sometimes, Poppy thought, it was hard to work out exactly how she felt about Freddie. She was devastated by the knowledge that he was married now and that she wouldn't be seeing him again – at least, not like that. But at other times there was a feeling of something like relief that she didn't have to worry any longer whether he loved her. He didn't, and she would have to deal with it as best she could.

Her subconscious didn't seem to have this same sensible approach, however, and several times she had a dream where Freddie turned up in her ward, dreadfully injured, and she glided to his side, put her hand on his forehead and somehow, miraculously, made him well again.

There was a strange contradiction, too, in Poppy's thoughts about what nursing in France would be like. The notion of travelling to a foreign country was very exciting, but when she considered the type of nursing she'd be doing, it was quite terrifying, too. In Netley's Hut 59 there were relatively few deaths – the men she cared for had proved robust enough to survive the journey to Blighty and, although they might need long-term care, were expected to live. Soon, however, she'd have to face the potentially stomach-turning injuries of men who'd come straight from the front line; men who had such horrendous wounds that nothing whatsoever could be done for them, except to try to give them a pain-free and peaceful end.

This matter was touched on a month later, when Poppy went to Devonshire House in London to be interviewed by one of the Red Cross matrons about her application to nurse abroad.

'You do realise, don't you, that in France you'll see more serious injuries than anything you've encountered in Netley?' her interviewer asked at the culmination of the meeting.

'Yes, I do,' Poppy replied firmly. She'd come a long way since her early training, when she'd been physically sick at the sight of a young soldier with his nose and part of his face burned, but had seen far worse since then. Before nursing, she'd never seen a naked male body – apart from her brother's, as a baby – but now she could bed-bath a man, or hand out and collect bedpans without a moment's hesitation or embarrassment. She felt that she could deal with almost anything.

'We urgently need more nursing VADs in France, but only the very best are chosen to work alongside our fighting men,' the matron commented, studying the paperwork on her desk. 'You've supplied me with an excellent reference, however, and Sister Kay has spoken to me personally about your suitability, so I have no doubt as to your capabilities. I therefore have pleasure in offering you a place at one of our base hospitals in France.'

Poppy, feeling a lump come into her throat, managed to croak out her thanks. VADs were usually upper-class girls who'd received a good education and had a private income, and Poppy didn't fit this specification at all. She'd been scared, too, that they'd want more information on her former job as a parlourmaid at Airey House and might contact Mrs de Vere, but it seemed that the nursing she'd done at Netley was sufficient to show them she was the sort of girl they wanted.

'We'll send details of your posting very soon, and you may not have much notice before you're expected to join the ship and cross the Channel. Take any leave owing to you now and make farewell visits to your people as soon as you can.'

'I will,' Poppy said, for she was intending to go and see her mother straight after the interview. 'Can I ask if it would be possible for me to work on a casualty clearing station? I've heard that's where the most good can be done.'

The matron shook her head. 'We don't allow VADs on casualty clearing stations, I'm afraid. Doctors and fully qualified nurses only.' As Poppy's face fell, the matron went on, 'You have to realise that the most dreadfully injured men are coming into the clearing stations straight from the trenches. We operate a triage system, so vital decisions have to be made immediately as to whether patients will benefit from urgent medical intervention, can afford to wait in line, or will be impossible to save. Sometimes operations are performed there and then, with fighting going on all around. A VAD – invaluable though you are – doesn't have the proper nursing qualifications to provide the doctors with the extra skills these situations need. Trained nurses in France are mostly older women who have more life experience.'

'I see,' Poppy said, disappointed.

'But your strengths, Pearson, seem to be in hands-on care, and there are many other ways you can be of use. In a base hospital you'll have a better chance of getting to know your patients, whereas at a clearing station the casualties are often like ships that pass in the night.' Matron signed some forms and put them in an envelope. 'I understand you're receiving a small amount of money each week from a family friend?'

Poppy nodded. 'My old schoolteacher, Miss Luttrell, kindly gives me a sum to cover my keep, uniform and so on.'

'That's very generous of her. I take it this will continue even though you'll receive a small salary now?'

'Miss Luttrell told me that the allowance is for the duration of the war – that I'm her war effort,' Poppy said, smiling. 'She was really keen for me to go on to college after school, but my mother couldn't afford to send me. Then Miss Luttrell came into some money and said that it was too late for college, but she'd help me become a VAD.'

'What an admirable idea!' Matron sealed the envelope. 'I'll send your details for processing now and you'll be hearing from us soon.'

They shook hands and Poppy, without thinking, bobbed a curtsey. Old habits died hard . . .

10th February 1916

Dear Miss Luttrell,

I am writing this on the train back to Netley. I've had my interview at Devonshire House and am very happy to tell you that the Matron-in-Charge has approved my application to work in France. I'll give you my new unit number and hospital details as soon as I know them. I'd hoped to come and see you, but when it came to it I only just had time to go to Wales to see my mother (who's still there with my aunt until the war's over). She's very pleased for me, but a little worried about how close I'll be to the fighting.

It's probably terribly immature of me, but I am very excited about going to France, a foreign country with a different language! My friend Matthews has been teasing me about the food she says I'll have to eat: nothing but frogs' legs and snails, apparently. I know already that the French version of Tommy is Poluis, *and I can say* hello, goodbye *and* thank you, *so that's a start.*

I wonder where I shall be sent? To the coast, I hope. Or, even more exciting, perhaps to Paris. I shall let you know. With all good wishes,

Poppy

'How did you get on?' Matthews asked the morning after Poppy's return to Netley. They were in the hostel canteen, filling up with enough porridge and toast to see them through the day.

Poppy smiled. 'I got in!'

'There. I knew you would.' There was a minute scraping of sugar left in the bowl and Matthews took this and sprinkled it on to her porridge, which looked grey and glutinous. She made a show of stirring it using both hands. 'This stuff is so thick you could stand a wooden post in the middle of it!'

'At Airey House,' Poppy said, 'the de Veres' cook used to make porridge with double cream and thick brown sugar. Sometimes she'd put the bowl under the grill and melt the top into toffee.'

Matthews sniffed. 'No food shortages there then.'

'None at all!' Poppy's thoughts drifted back to those mornings when she'd take the silver porringer into the Airey House breakfast room and find herself alone with Freddie. He'd give her one of those looks and she'd usually drop something or find herself unable to speak.

'Hey!' Matthews clapped her hands. 'You're dreaming about him again, aren't you? Stop! He's an utter beast and that's all there is to it. Think of poor Miss Cardew, if you must think of someone; the boy she loves was carrying on with someone else even as she was planning their society wedding.'

Poppy nodded. 'I know all that, but . . .'

'Let's think about – talk about – someone else,' Matthews said. 'Like your brother.'

'I really don't think talking about Billy will cheer me up.'

'No, but where is he? Still in Dottyville or has he rejoined his regiment?'

'I don't know,' Poppy said. 'And neither does Ma.' Finishing the porridge, she poured herself a pile of cornflakes and added some milk. There being no sugar left in the bowl, she began to crunch her way through them.

'Your ma still doesn't know about . . . ?'

Poppy shook her head. After Billy's regiment was sent to the front, he'd been shipped back to England and admitted to Netley with a gunshot wound to his foot – a wound which had proved to be self-inflicted. Doctor Michael Archer had kindly pulled strings on their behalf and, after having Billy's leg seen to, managed to get him sent to a hospital in Scotland, nicknamed 'Dottyville' by its inmates. Here he'd received treatment for the condition known as neurasthenia and recently renamed shell shock. Poppy knew that Billy was extremely lucky not to have been court-martialled for his actions. The punishment for cowardice under fire was severe – he could have been shot at dawn.

'Ma knows he was injured, but she doesn't know how it happened.' Poppy sighed. 'I hope she never finds out. She'd be so ashamed of him.'

There was a moment's silence, then Matthews said, 'And yet . . .'

Poppy looked at her questioningly.

'And yet, when you think about it, it takes a certain bravery to shoot yourself in the foot, doesn't it? I don't think I could do it.'

'You're just saying that to make me feel better,' Poppy said.

Matthews shrugged.

Poppy had mixed feelings about the letter from Billy which came a week or so later.

A farmyard nr edinbro

Hiya Sis,
Well they have let me out and i have a certificat to show that i am as sane as the next man – which if this war is still going on is not very sane at all. I have a month when i will be working on a farm jest outside of edinbro and then they say i will be returning to duty. I do not no what

this will be like. I am feeling alright now but if they are thinking of sending me to the front i don't know what i will do. I am not going back in those trenches with rats mud and dead bodys no matter what.

No wonder they call it dottyville. The peeple in charge are as mad as the inmates or madder if that is possibel. They row between themselves about what is the right treatment for a chap. Some say bedrest and quiet. Some say shout at them and make noises to frighten them so they will get used to it. They take picktures so there is a record of what they do. Mind you, your doctor pal did a good job in getting me here as i am about the only private. I think all the others are officers. Anyone would think it is only the nobs get troubled in there heads and the rest of us poor blighters jest have to put up with it. I will write to ma and tell her i am going to work on a farm – she will like that. You can write to me here – it will be forwarded on.

Love from your brother Billy x x x

Chapter Three

Poppy paused at the foot of the gangplank of HMS *Paris Belle* and looked back over the bustling dockyard. She had a sudden feeling of panic – suppose this was the last time she saw England! Suppose the ship was torpedoed by a U-boat, or bombed by German aeroplanes, or hit a mine? Suppose she drowned and never saw her home and family ever again? It would break her mother's heart, her little sisters would forget all about her, and all that would remain of her would be a photograph on the mantel-piece, fading gently year by year.

My country, England! she thought. A wave of some-thing like nostalgia swept over her and she was groping in her bag for a handkerchief when she suddenly got shoved in the back by a soldier's hefty kitbag.

'Hey. Sorry, ma'am!' a voice said in a rich drawl. 'Didn't see you there.'

'My fault!' Poppy said, and then as the man apologised again, added that it didn't matter in the slightest. 'But, excuse me, you're Australian, aren't you?'

'Nope,' the soldier said with a grin.

'American?'

He shook his head.

'Canadian!' Poppy said.

He nodded. 'Right! The difference is,' he continued, 'that Canada and Australia are in the war, the Yanks aren't. Not yet. Although a lot of their medics are over as volunteers.'

'Hey! What's the hold-up?' someone shouted from further down the gangplank.

Poppy mumbled an apology, smiled at the soldier and ran up the last dozen steps of the plank on to the ship.

When she got off this ship, she thought, she would be in France. A foreign country. They ate strange food there and, according to the magazines Poppy had seen, dressed very stylishly. They had different money, a different language, and it was all going to be very odd.

She found herself a wooden slatted seat on the top deck. Her mother had told her to stay outside in the fresh air as long as possible, and if she felt sick, to stare at the horizon and chew a piece of ginger. Where she could get such a thing, her mother hadn't said.

The journey, she'd been told, was about twelve hours, provided the ship didn't have to go off course to avoid German shipping. She carried troops, equipment and possibly, for all Poppy knew, guns and ammunition, so could not sail under the patronage of the Red Cross. They would disembark at a well known French port, although, because of security, Poppy hadn't been told which one. There she'd receive notification as to the hospital she'd be working at.

It was windy out on deck and Poppy did up the top button of her cloak, jammed her winter-uniform felt hat tightly over her fair hair, checked that the lock of the rather battered suitcase she'd borrowed from Ma was still holding, and closed her eyes.

She'd had a very emotional morning, first of all saying goodbye to Matthews, Jameson and the rest of her VAD friends at the hostel, then – even worse – bidding fare-well to the patients of Hut 59. The girl who was to be her replacement had started two days before, a pretty girl with dark eyes and hair long enough to plait right round her head who'd already been nicknamed Indian Queen by the boys. Poppy also had to bear Private Sharp telling her that he thought the new VAD looked like Lillian Gish, the glamorous movie star.

She felt ashamed at any petty feelings of jealousy, however, when the boys brought out the autograph book they'd made for her. Every man on the ward who had use of his arms had written something: something funny or sentimental or both. Three of them had written poems. Somehow, too, they'd found out her first name and the book's pages were liberally strewn with poppies in scarlet crayon.

Then there were the thoughtful presents: a brooch made from a piece of shrapnel which had been removed from Private Taylor's back, a white lawn handkerchief embroidered with Private Tippett's regimental badge and several hand-carved wooden figures. Poppy started to read the contents of the autograph book, but faltered at the first poem, which declared:

> *She cheers us when we're lonely,*
> *She bandages us when we fall,*
> *Our Very Adorable Darling*
> *Is the loveliest VAD of all.*

Already feeling emotional, Poppy nearly broke down at this, and decided to leave the reading of the book until she was on her own. Sniffing, she'd thanked everyone and promised to send them messages care of Moffat, the other long-term VAD in the ward. There was no sign of Michael Archer, which was a little disappointing, but she thought he might have received his orders and already be Out There.

The *Paris Belle* slowly filled up with passengers. They were mostly in uniform: doctors, nurses and VADs, orderlies, bandsmen and small groups of men intending to rejoin their regiments after convalescence. Most men were wearing the khaki of the British soldier, but there were other Allied uniforms in different shades of grey or khaki, and a few French soldiers in very smart grey-blue trench coats.

As Poppy sat watching the work going on along the quayside, huge crates came on board containing mail bags. This caused her to think how many there were and how desperately each letter was longed for – which in turn led to thoughts of Freddie again, and his last letter assuring her that there was nothing between him and Miss Cardew. Fancy her being so stupid as to believe him!

Then another thought struck her: suppose he hadn't actually gone through with the wedding? The newspaper report had said that it would take place quietly on New Year's Day, but what if, once on leave, Freddie had decided that it was Poppy whom he really loved? And now – well, now she was fleeing the country and he'd never be able to find her! This notion only occupied her for a few moments, however, until she faced the fact that Christmas had been more than two months ago and even the slowest writer in the world would have found a way to get an important message through in all that time.

Far below where Poppy was sitting, a dozen horses came on board, shaking their manes and twitching their tails. Following them came crates containing tinned food and medical supplies, and then such diverse objects as pigeons in cages, bicycles, tin baths, inner tubes for car wheels, crates of beer and piles of new kitbags were loaded into the vastness of the hold. Finally, the great doors were shut, the gangway removed and a shout was given of 'Anchors away!'.

The ship hooted loudly enough to make Poppy put her hands over her ears and they were off, leaving the crowds on the quayside waving, crying and hurraying in equal measure.

The ship slid along the side of the quay and Poppy got a quick look at some of those who'd gathered to wave goodbye to their soldier boys: mothers and fathers, sweethearts, sisters, children. And pets . . .

Someone on the deck below Poppy was shouting 'Good dog! Easy, Blue!' to a sprightly Border collie on a short lead who was evidently barking his misery at his master going off to war. The animal carried on non-stop and then, as the ship began to turn herself ready to move out of the harbour, suddenly jerked the lead away from the hand of the woman who held it and jumped into the water.

The woman screamed, the people about her shouted, and Poppy heard a frantic 'No! Go back, Blue!' from the dog's owner on the ship.

Blue took no notice, however, and was seen to be swimming frantically after the ship in an effort to catch her up. Those on the shore shouted an alert, which was taken up by those on board the *Paris Belle* who'd witnessed the event, and in a few moments everyone in sight was yelling and pointing at the small black and white animal doggy-paddling through the waves.

After perhaps a minute, with the ship about to leave the safety of the home port, her engines stopped. The collie swam on and, to loud cheers, a small rowing boat was lowered on ropes from the *Paris Belle* into the water. This held three people, who were – the word quickly spread – a seaman, the dog's owner and a vet going out to Flanders to tend to horses. The seaman pulled hard on the oars to reach the dog. The collie was picked up and hauled on board by its owner, and subsequently held upside down by its rear legs by the vet so it could choke out water, all to loud cheers from those on ship and shore.

Once they were out of the harbour and on the open sea, Poppy discovered something new about herself, something she'd had no idea about before: she suffered from seasickness.

Queasy and dry-mouthed but trying to ignore it, she spoke to two young women, trained nurses, about where they were heading and heard that they'd both been on leave from a tented hospital in Calais. 'Absolutely everything is under canvas,' they told her. 'Operating theatres, dining hall, kitchens, nurses' bedrooms and bathrooms. We love it – except when it rains.' They went off and Poppy was just about to approach a girl she perceived from her uniform to be another VAD, when she realised that walking on a floor which first sloped one way, then the next, was making her feel quite ill.

Feeling the cold and shivering by now, she went inside, into what once had been a grand ballroom, and looked for somewhere to sit. The more she walked around, however, the worse she felt. In the end, utterly nauseous, she sat down on the grand central staircase, rested her head on her knees and prayed for the journey to France to be over as quickly as possible.

A short while later, word spread that a canteen had opened one deck up, and Poppy, thinking a hot drink might do her good, got to her feet. She was only halfway across the room, however, when she felt horribly sick and had to rush into the lavatories.

'Not got your sea legs?' a girl in a St John nurse's uniform asked sympathetically when she came out.

Poppy shook her head. 'My mother told me to chew a piece of ginger, but she didn't actually tell me where to get it and . . .' But the mere thought of eating anything made her feel so ghastly that she had to turn around and lurch back into the lavatory again.

When Poppy came out, she sat herself down on a bench on deck, stared ahead resolutely and prayed she would see land very soon . . .

Chapter Four

20th February 1916

Dearest Ma,

I am on French soil. I am a Continental traveller. How sophisticated I am!

I wasn't feeling so good a few hours back, mind you. Gosh, seasickness is ghastly. I've never felt so ill or been so glad to get anywhere in all my life. When the ship reached Boulogne-sur-Mer and I walked unsteadily down that gangplank – green in the face, I'm sure, and with my legs all wobbly beneath me – I felt like kneeling and kissing the ground.

I am sitting with a selection of other young women, all nurses and VADs, in a building which looks like a log cabin. This, I've been told, is a harbour master's office, and we are all waiting to see which hospitals we are to *be sent to. I hope and pray that it doesn't mean a further sea trip round the coast. I think I'd run away!*

I'm sure you will have heard from Billy by now. The lucky boy has been sent to a farm in Scotland to help out with the livestock before he's reassigned to a new regiment. This will mean freezing early mornings and very hard work, but it's better than being on the firing line.

I will finish now by sending you and the girls all my love. I will leave a space on the back of the envelope to put my new hospital address so you can write to me.
All my love and a kiss for Mary and Jane,

Poppy

PS If there are great big black lines on this letter it will mean that certain words have been deleted by the censor.

Poppy, still waiting in the wooden shed but happy to be away from the ship, longed to know what France looked like. All she'd seen so far was a part of the dockyard very much like the one they'd left in Southampton. As they'd gone from the ship to the shore, however, she'd heard the thunder of far away guns and seen streaks of fire lighting the sky. Wherever that was, she thought, men were fighting, inflicting horrible injuries on each other, breathing their last. It was going on right then, while she sat in this closeted room. Now, just a train ride away, men were blinding each other, mangling limbs, tearing flesh and bleeding their life blood into the earth.

It made her feel quite desperate. It seemed so primitive, like something a Stone Age man would do. Surely, she thought, there must be a better way of settling disputes than that?

There were lamps burning in the cabin, which made the room hot and stuffy and gave off a strong smell of paraffin. When Poppy loosened her cloak, the young woman beside her, who'd been making half-hearted small talk, suddenly noticed the mid-blue of her cotton dress and looked rather surprised.

'Oh, you're just a VAD,' she said.

Poppy, immediately on the defensive at the word *just*, glanced at the other girl, who was wearing the darker blue dress of a trained nurse. 'That's right. I did my training at Southampton.'

'Are you a domestic?'

'No, I'm a nurse.'

'Hardly a nurse, are you, dear?' said the young woman. 'I studied for two years to be able to call myself that.'

'Really?' Inside, Poppy bubbled with fury; outside, she managed to smile. 'I realise I'm not fully qualified, but my ward sister at Netley was pleased enough with my work to suggest I come over to France.'

'I suppose they have to take what they can get,' came the reply. Poppy, quietly fuming, didn't say anything and the girl carried on, 'My aunt is Matron-in-Charge at a hospital in Étaples and they're crying out for more properly qualified nurses. But that's not what I'm going to do – I'm going to be trained to work an X-ray machine.'

'How interesting,' Poppy said in a deadpan voice which revealed she didn't really think it was.

'They're marvellous things! One can see at a glance which bones are broken and which aren't. Saves an awful lot of trouble.' She gave Poppy another look. 'I don't suppose you've seen one.'

'I have, actually,' Poppy said. 'We had them in Netley. But I shouldn't care to work one. I'd much rather be hands on with my work.' So saying, she moved slightly on the bench so as to leave a small gap between the two of them.

She knew that some fully qualified nurses resented VADs, especially as injured soldiers hardly seemed to know the difference between them, calling them all 'nurse' and thinking they were all angels. Poppy, however, had encountered no nastiness or segregation from the trained nursing staff at Netley – in fact, the very opposite. Sister Kay and Nurse Gallagher had gone out of their way to teach her the correct bandaging techniques for different types of wounds and breaks, and indeed most other things concerning the care and welfare of an injured man.

The conversation between the two most definitely at an end, Poppy stood up, stretched and sat down again.

Another half-hour went by and, though her eyes felt itchy and heavy, she didn't want to fall asleep in case her head slipped on to the shoulder of Miss Hoity-toity alongside her. In the end, she put her suitcase on the floor, sat down beside it and went to sleep resting her head against it.

Another ship docked but Poppy, exhausted from the journey and the travel-sickness, was fast asleep and didn't hear more girls arriving in the room.

At eight o'clock in the morning, two VADs came in with a rattling tea trolley and Poppy woke to find the number of nurses there had doubled. Soon after this, she was informed that she'd been assigned to a base hospital just outside the port of Boulogne, known as Petit Boulogne. She was particularly pleased – firstly because it wasn't Étaples and she wouldn't have to travel onward with Miss Hoity-toity, and secondly because she would be travelling to the hospital on the top of a London omnibus, one of a group of buses on loan to the army.

Boulogne and the surrounding area had once been fashionable holiday places, but since the war nearly all the hotels, restaurants and public buildings had been taken over by the military. Most of their original inhabitants had gone, and the shopkeepers who were left made their living selling food, cigarettes and souvenirs to passing soldiers.

The hospital Poppy would be working in had previously been a casino. Boulogne offered what was possibly the fastest sea route across to England and had train lines which ran from the central station not only further around the coast, but also towards the front line, so casualties could be put on a train close to the battlefield and brought to a base hospital quickly. Here they could be treated and either returned to the front line, or possibly – what they all craved – stabilised, ready to travel home to England on a 'Blighty ticket'.

On giving her name to an orderly, she was taken down into the basement to rooms which had once been used for storage but were now converted into small bedrooms or cubicles, each one separated from the others by screens on wheels. Each cubicle had hooks with coat hangers, a small chest of drawers with a lamp on top, and a plain wooden chair. The sheets and blankets for the narrow single beds stood, neatly folded, waiting to be put on, and Poppy did this as soon as she'd unpacked, knowing she was bound to be too tired later, after a day on the wards.

The bedcover was faded and patched, but clean enough. Having made up the bed and thinking to herself that it looked quite inviting, Poppy, still feeling the after-effects of the journey, lay down for a moment before unpacking. She closed her eyes and, without meaning to, went straight off to sleep.

In this way she started off very much on the wrong foot with Sister Sherwood of Ward 5, who'd requested a VAD and two trained nurses from HQ at Devonshire

House, but had been given only a VAD. This VAD, unbelievably, had had the audacity to fall asleep as soon as she'd arrived.

'I'm so sorry,' Poppy said. It was two hours later, after she had been woken by a nurse despatched in search of her and taken into Sister Sherwood's presence. 'I didn't mean to fall asleep. I just tried out the bed and . . .'

But Sister Sherwood was writing a letter and didn't look up.

Poppy waited politely for her to finish. When Sister's letter had been folded and the envelope addressed, she added, 'I didn't get any sleep on the ship, you see, and I kept being sick and was just so exhausted that –'

'As exhausted as these soldiers are after weeks in trenches on the front line?' Sister Sherwood interrupted, gesturing down the ward. 'As sick as they are, as deprived of sleep as they are?'

Poppy hesitated. 'No, of course not,' she said, very quickly adding, 'Sister.'

'I will not have anyone in my ward who is less than fully committed. You have a strange idea of nursing if you think you can go to sleep before attending to your patients. Haven't you had any training at all, girl? Don't you know the men come first at all times?'

Poppy, knocked sideways by this onslaught, didn't say a word. The worst thing had happened, she thought. She'd not only be working for a misery-guts of a sister, but she'd got off on the wrong foot with her.

'If you're not going to pull your weight or you intend to bring my ward into disrepute in any other way, you may turn round now and go straight home.'

Poppy, stung to tears, blinked hard to disperse them. Sister Sherwood? More like Sister Shrew . . .

'You already know the rules, Pearson. Just see you obey them. Now, perhaps you can start by taking round the men's water jugs – if that's not too much trouble for you.'

It was not a good start.

Chapter Five

Ward 5 in the casino hospital seemed much more subdued than Ward 59 in Netley. At Netley the boys were always playing tricks on each other, teasing Poppy and the other nurses or singing ditties with dubious meanings, but on Ward 5 there were none of these high jinks.

At first Poppy put this down to the forbidding presence of Sister Shrew, but after a while realised that that was only part of it; it was mainly because the boys in the casino hospital were in worse shape than the Netley boys. Most patients arrived straight from a casualty clearing station, and once in a ward would sleep, have their smashed limbs set or amputated, and receive treatment for any other wounds or illnesses. Only when their conditions were considered stable would they be moved on. Very rarely had men arrived in Southampton straight from the battlefield, covered in mud and with their wounds untouched, as they sometimes did in Boulogne.

In its favour, Ward 5 was considerably more glamorous than Hut 59, for it had once been one of the casino's gaming rooms. A bevy of draped mythic goddesses were painted on the ceiling, there were mirrors of gilt, and lavish depictions of the twelve months of the year were hung on the walls.

The beds, running in four straight lines down from top to bottom, dominated the room, however. These, and the metal lockers and blue counterpanes, were standard War Office issue. Sister Sherwood didn't have Sister Kay's powers of acquisition as far as pyjamas were concerned, either. With Sister Kay it had been a matter of honour that all her patients wore neat and tidy red- or blue-striped flannelette pyjamas, the tops always matching the bottoms. Those worn by the boys of Ward 5, although always clean, were second hand and showed enough variety of stripes, colours and checks to make a patchwork quilt.

Poppy was to find that the boys in the beds – however mismatched their pyjamas – were every bit as grateful, thankful and stalwart as they'd been in Netley. The ward was primarily for amputees, with its current occupants including eight double amputees and one triple amputee, but nearly all of these men had something else wrong in addition: a stomach wound, a head injury, a smashed-up shoulder, pneumonia, or a face that had been slashed with a bayonet.

The unfortunate man with three limbs missing was Private Norman, who was waiting for his wounds to heal a little more before being despatched to the Rehabilitation Centre at Roehampton, where he would be fitted with prosthetic limbs. But he needed a considerable amount of treatment first, for not only did he have one leg and two arms missing below the elbow, but he was covered with shrapnel wounds and had also contracted trench foot, which had led to two of his smallest toes being removed from his remaining foot. The irony of this, he told everyone, was that his other foot, the one which had been amputated, had been completely trench foot free.

'Fancy losing the good 'un and keeping the mangy one!' he remarked to Poppy. 'Where's the fairness in that? Why couldn't Jerry have shot off the bad foot if he wanted to shoot anything?'

But he was a cheerful young man and, being the only triple amputee, was made quite a fuss of in the ward. Even those who'd been unfortunate enough to lose two limbs couldn't complain when confronted with someone who'd lost three. If the other men received food parcels from home, they'd always see he got a few squares of chocolate or a slice of cake.

Two weeks after reaching the Casino Hospital, Poppy had her first afternoon off and found time to write to her friend.

Casino Hospital,
Nr Boulogne-sur-Mer,
France

28th February 1916

Dear Matthews,
How are you? Are you really busy at Netley? Writing to you using your second name looks strange, but when I put 'Dear Essie' at the top of this letter it didn't seem as if it was really you I was writing to.

I've now spent my first few days in a big military hospital – it's nicknamed the 'Casino' (which it used to be) – and have to tell you that I am not very happy. For a start, the weather here is atrocious. Everyone at home said that the weather in France would be better than in England, but it's not. It is absolutely pelting with rain and has been since I arrived. Anyway, that wouldn't be so bad if hospital life was all right, but that's awful, too. I have an absolute beast of a woman as my superior – Sister Sherwood, or Sister Shrew as I've renamed her. She is the meanest, coldest, most shrewish person you could ever meet and not at all the sort of woman anyone would want as their ward sister. I didn't get off to a good start with her because I accidentally fell asleep the morning I arrived, but although I really apologised, she'd already made up her mind that I was a dead loss.

The end result is this: I'm not allowed to do ANYTHING. That is, I'm not allowed to do anything that a ten-year-old child wouldn't be able to do blind-folded. I can lay trays, fill jugs and tidy lockers and – oh yes, she doesn't mind this – take round and collect bedpans, but nothing else. Of course, there are some horrifically injured men here, but I've had plenty of experience of horrific injuries and think I'm now quite proficient at cleaning wounds, packing them out and re-bandaging. I could be useful giving injections and applying poultices, bed-bathing men with legs in traction and lots of other things, but Sister doesn't allow me to do any of these.

Yesterday Private Ridge complained to me that his arm was bandaged so tightly that he kept getting very painful pins and needles so, Sister Shrew being busy on a doctor's round, I cut the bandage, ready to apply a looser dressing. But before I could put it on, S.S. arrived and tore a strip off me in front of Private Ridge and all the doctors. She was simply horrible, wanting to know how I had the impudence, how I jolly well dared to touch anyone on her ward! There are two trained nurses on the ward and neither of them spoke up for me (though I can't say I blame them, faced with her) and two VADs, both of whom are so terrified of S.S. that their voices go all squeaky when they speak to her.

The boys here are as lovely as those in Netley, even though their injuries are mostly worse. They are endlessly patient and thoughtful. If S.S. has had a go at me, they whisper, 'I see the wind's in the east today,' and other things to make me laugh.

It's very strange to think that the war is going on just down the road from here. Lying in bed at night I can hear the guns going off and bombs exploding and then, usually within twenty-four hours, new casualties are admitted. I always wonder which particular explosion caused which horrendous injury.

I am doing my best to stop mooning over Freddie in the face of such real pain and loss. It is still hard, though – every time I see a squadron of soldiers in the square I can't help looking to see which regiment they're from. I ask myself what I'd do if I ever saw him again and like to think that I'd be calm and restrained, that I'd congratulate him on his marriage then just pass him by, but . . .

Oh, do think of coming over here, Matthews! I know it's really selfish, but I do miss having someone to talk to. Your affectionate friend,

Poppy

Going out to post the letter, Poppy wondered what she was going to do about Sister Shrew. She was used to red tape and tedious War Office ways, but not to someone constantly breathing down her neck, criticising her and tut-tutting in the background. Why, even when she'd been a parlourmaid she'd been allowed to work on her own initiative! Tall and commanding, Sister Shrew often stalked up behind Poppy, spoke to her sharply and made her jump, or stood on the other side of the bed to where Poppy was working, a silent presence, waiting (hoping, Poppy thought) for her to drop the scissors or fail to get the lid off a tub of boracic powder.

Of course, in some ways it was easier not to have the responsibility of changing the boys' bandages, cleansing their wounds and managing the intricate pulley affairs that kept their shattered legs straight. However, these most difficult parts of nursing were, in a strange way, also the best and when Poppy felt she was doing the most good. The giving out and collecting of bedpans, the filling of water jugs and the putting on of clean pillowslips was not fulfilling. She missed helping the boys cope with their injuries, missed their thankfulness when she eased their pain and the moment when, after carefully bandaging a man, he'd sigh in contentment and say, 'Thanks, nurse. That feels much better.'

One positive thing was that she was always busy, which meant less time dwelling on Freddie de Vere. In fact, on this first afternoon off, she was congratulating herself on not thinking of him all day when, going down to her room, she found a letter from England with Molly's name and address on the back.

Molly had been a maid at the de Vere family home, too, though she'd had no idea about the romance which had been going on between her friend and the de Veres' youngest son. Looking at the front of the envelope, Poppy realised that the letter must have been some time on its journey to France, for it bore several different addresses, including Netley Hospital, Devonshire House and even the Welsh address of Poppy's ma.

22 Bartram Buildings,
Mayfield,
Herts

Dear Poppy,
I thought you would be interested in the enclosed cutting from the local paper. What a pity it didn't happen when we were still working at Airey House – we would have been allowed to watch everything and maybe take a glass or two to toast the happy couple!

I am still in the munitions factory and have been promoted so I am now a line manager. My dad says I am doing a man's job, but I am not yet getting a man's pay! Mayfield has been quite depleted of men and when I've been to the pictures or to a music hall, there are twice as many women as men in the audience. At the town hall dance this year, we girls had to waltz with each other. It was like being back at school.

Since then, I have managed to find myself a young man and we are officially walking out together. His name is Albert Higgins and he is a topping chap whose dad owns the boot shop down the high street. They both have exemption certificates because they are the official repair centre for army boots when the boys come home on leave. Albert also repairs kitbag straps and leather belts (and handbags, not that the army wants those) so he is jolly useful.

Anyway, enjoy the enclosed and do write and let me know how things are with you.
All love,

Molly x

Poppy struggled not to look at the newspaper cutting, for she knew already what it must be. Even as she urged herself to tear it up, however, she was removing it from the envelope and unfolding it. She took a breath.

Second Lieutenant de Vere marries Society Beauty, said the caption at the top. The small photograph underneath was not a good one and, because it was taken some distance away, the expression on Freddie's face was not clear. Next to Freddie were his mother and father, with Miss Cardew's family on the other side and, of course, his bride, wearing a slim, fitting white silk dress with a train which swirled about her feet and a sparkling tiara on her shiny bobbed hair. Underneath the photograph it said:

The last time the de Vere family had reason to meet at the family's chapel in Mayfield, it was on the sad occasion of a memorial service following the death of the eldest de Vere son, Jasper, who perished in the brave service of his country. This time the occasion was a joyous one as Second Lieutenant Frederick de Vere, of the Duke of Greystock's Regiment, married his childhood sweetheart,

Miss Philippa Imogen Cardew, and these two noble families became united. Miss Cardew is pictured wearing a pure silk gown and the family diamond tiara. There will not be a honeymoon as the groom is on active service with his regiment somewhere in France. This newspaper wishes the young couple every happiness.

Poppy stared at the photograph for some time. There was absolutely no chance now of pretending to herself that the wedding might not have happened, because here they were, the perfect couple, in black and white.

Society Beauty, she thought. As if she, Poppy, could ever have been called that! Two noble families united – how would the de Veres have coped, being united with the family of their parlourmaid? Why, she didn't even own a diamond tiara . . .

Chapter Six

S he would not cry. She would not. If she could bear the sight of Private Toone, blinded by gas, trying to write to his wife ... If she could stand seeing Private Norman, one stump of a hand on his bedhead and the other on his locker, grimly trying to balance himself on his only leg, then surely she could bear a broken heart? She just had to tell herself it would never have worked out between her and Freddie. They could never have been together. Never, never, never ...

She screwed up the newspaper cutting and threw it in the bin, then after a moment retrieved it, smoothed it out and, without looking at it again, placed it between the pages of a medical dictionary and put the book in the back of her chest of drawers. It would be a test, she thought. When she felt she could look at the photograph without feeling she was being cut in half, then she'd know she didn't care about him any more. *Then* she would throw the cutting away.

She desperately wished she had someone to talk to about it: Matthews, preferably. Matthews would be in a fury about the whole thing, say that Freddie had behaved in a beastly rotten way and Poppy was lucky to be rid of him. Then Poppy would have a good weep, admit that Matthews was right and feel a lot better.

There was no one to tell, though – certainly no one in Ward 5. She couldn't bother the trained nurses with something of that nature – they were much too respectable and proper – besides, they were entirely concerned with their patients. They would not understand how such an unsuitable liaison had happened in the first place. The two VADs in the ward weren't the type to confide in, either. They were very well-to-do and, being single ladies well over forty, couldn't be expected to remember what it was like to have your heart broken. More than likely, they would think it shocking that someone of her standing could ever aim so high as Freddie de Vere. Anyway, Poppy thought, finally dismissing them as confidantes, they were devoted to Sister Shrew and no one who was devoted to *that* person could ever become her friend.

She looked round the gloomy basement room and decided she ought to go for a walk. So far, she'd seen very little of this foreign country she'd been so excited about working in, for, like everyone there, she worked long hours and gave up her half-day off if they were busy with new admissions. Today, though, she definitely felt the need to get out, go somewhere, do something.

The hospital was hardly more than a stone's throw from Boulogne-sur-Mer's docks and Poppy began to walk in that direction. Dodging the lorries, Red Cross trucks, army jeeps, private ambulances and a horse-drawn bus, and arriving in the main square, she found the whole place full of Tommies, army officers and nurses. Looking about, it seemed that the whole town had been turned over to the war. Some places which had once been shops now had their windows white-washed and were being occupied by Belgian refugees who'd fled from the German troops occupying their villages; other units had been turned into bars and cafés for off-duty Tommies. Some shops were boarded up and being used as storage space for items destined to be transported to the front as and when they were needed: tents, stretchers, crates of tinned food, munitions, blankets . . . all the requirements of an army on the move.

Finding a small kiosk open, Poppy bought some souvenir postcards showing the promenade in its heyday (with floaty-skirted women walking along the beach with lace-trimmed parasols) to send to her sisters, and also a keepsake for herself, a metal mug made from a tin which had once contained condensed milk. The boys in the trenches had taken to making these mugs whilst waiting for the call to fight.

Other than these mugs, some week-old English news-papers and a selection of pilfered German army badges, there wasn't a great deal in the shops – certainly none of the stylish clothes that Poppy had been hoping to see.

Even food had to be hunted down because army regiments, passing through on their way either to the front or to a different location, would clear shelves of chocolate, cakes, bread and biscuits. Basic medical requirements like plasters, bandages, headache pills and anything that could be fitted into a kitbag were also quickly snapped up, either by Tommies or by one of the small private hospitals that had sprung up in the area.

Walking through the square and along the promenade, Poppy passed a score of luxury hotels which had been turned into hospitals: the Hotel de Luxe, the Savoy, the Palais de Bain. A dog cart, pulled by two strong Alsatian dogs, went by with an old woman sitting in it, and Poppy was marvelling at the novelty of this when she heard a man's voice calling.

'Pearson! I say, over here, Pearson!'

Immediately presuming it was Freddie, for he was still not far from her mind, Poppy felt her legs go to jelly. She didn't want to see him yet! Well, she didn't want to see him at all, but especially not until she'd worked out what she was going to say; what cutting remark, what withering put-down or sarcastic comment she would fell him with. Turning, she saw that it wasn't Freddie de Vere – who, anyway, had always called her Poppy – but Doctor Michael Archer, last seen in the kitchen of Hut 59 on Christmas Day.

'Pearson. How good to see you!' It had seemed, Poppy thought later, as if he'd been about to put out his arm to hug her, but halfway there he changed it into a handshake. 'I've been wondering where you might have ended up.'

Poppy allowed her arm to be shaken vigorously, and said, 'I'm in Ward 5 at the Casino, along the promenade.' It was good to see him too, she thought. Lovely to see a familiar and friendly face from home – and a great relief that it wasn't Freddie's. 'Where are you stationed?'

'A few miles inland, at a casualty clearing station.'

'I asked to go to a clearing station.' She shrugged. 'But – I know – no VADs allowed.'

Michael shook his head. 'Qualified sisters and theatre staff only.'

'Is it gruelling?'

'Pretty gory, yes. And we're taking in casualties day and night now. They've just started to come in from Verdun, too.'

Poppy looked at him questioningly. 'But that's mostly a French–German battle?'

He nodded. 'The thing is, there have been so many men injured that the French hospitals down there can't take them all. They're coming along in train-loads. Your hospital will be getting casualties from Verdun soon – that's if they haven't got them already.'

There was an awkward silence before Poppy spoke again. 'So what are you doing here now?'

'Well, there was a lull in admissions, one of the hospital cars was free and I had a couple of hours off, so they sent me here to try and hunt down some decent fodder for the overworked doctors.' He lifted a big canvas shopping bag. 'All we've had for the past three days has been bully beef and tinned peas, and tonight we'll probably be working all night.'

'I saw potatoes for sale in a laundry behind the town hall,' Poppy offered.

His face brightened. 'I was really hoping for eggs – they're number one on my list – but potatoes are a good start. Where's the town hall?'

'In the square, though actually it's no longer the town hall, but a dental hospital. I had to take a patient with a shattered jaw over there yesterday to have all his teeth out.'

He raised his eyebrows. 'Things are all downside up, eh? A laundry selling potatoes, a town hall that's a dental hospital, a casino where there's no gambling.'

'Except with men's lives,' Poppy said.

He grinned. 'Very perceptive, Pearson. Or can I call you by your first name now we're out of England?'

'I shouldn't think so for a minute,' Poppy said, thinking of Sister Sherwood.

'I suppose that young man of yours wouldn't approve.'

'No . . .' Poppy was about to say that she didn't have a young man – probably never *had* had one – but for some reason thought better of it. No, let Doctor Archer think she had someone, then he would stay at arm's length. 'No, he probably wouldn't.'

'And are you enjoying France?'

Poppy shook her head slowly. 'Not . . . awfully much.'

'Oh dear. I'm sorry to hear that.'

At the sympathy in his voice, Poppy's eyes welled up. 'I know I'm probably being a complete ninny,' she said, 'but it's my ward sister. I can't seem to get on with her.'

'No?'

'It's not at all like I thought it would be here. I don't feel useful. I just spend my time folding sheets, washing bedpans and laying up trays. I mean, I don't mind doing those things, but I want to do other things as well! I'm not allowed to change bandages, pack wounds, apply poultices or do any of the medical tasks I did at Netley.' She suddenly remembered she was speaking to a doctor – an officer – and blushed. 'Sorry, I'm being really unprofessional. We're just supposed to do whatever we're asked without complaining, aren't we? It says so in the VADs' instruction book.'

'Never mind about that,' he said. 'We're friends. And if you can't tell your friend something . . .'

'I don't think VADs are allowed to have friends.'

'Nonsense!'

Poppy managed a smile.

'But anyway, how's that brother of yours?'

Poppy made a so-so gesture with her hand. 'The last I heard, he was out of Dottyville and working on a farm near Edinburgh. He sounds more or less back to his old self.'

He nodded. 'Good. Let's hope he gets stationed somewhere out of the way where he doesn't feel he –'

What he was going to say Poppy didn't find out, however, because there was a sudden shouting and cheering in the street, a loud grinding, rumbling noise then, from around the corner, a large, awkward-looking vehicle appeared, part lorry and part tractor, with a pipe like an elephant's trunk sticking out at the front. A handful of local children was running behind it, all shouting, and someone had hung a branch of green bay leaves around its turret in some semblance of a wreath of honour. The vehicle went slowly past them, and Poppy saw a Tommy sitting in the turret, waving to each side of him.

'Judging by the cheering, it's one of ours,' she said. 'But whatever is it?'

'Well, I've only seen a drawing of one before now, but I believe they're calling it a land-ship or a tank. We're going to have about a dozen of them.'

'What will they do?'

'Kill an awful lot of Germans,' he said wryly. 'They can knock over barriers, go through barbed wire and pass right across the trenches. Nothing can touch them.'

'But what an extraordinary-looking thing!'

'They have machine guns and a stack of grenades on board, and the pipe affair on the top is a cannon.'

'Sounds scary,' Poppy said.

'Exactly, and now that I've seen one I can visualise the damage it will cause to human flesh,' he said. 'Damage that you and I will have to deal with.'

'But it's ours.'

'Oh, make no mistake, the Germans will use them too. They're probably copying the blueprints right now – that's what they have spies for.'

Poppy's eyes followed the strange-looking vehicle as it trundled down the road. When she turned back to Michael, she saw that he was looking at her with a half-smile on his face.

'You know it's important in a war to maintain morale,' he said.

'So they say . . .'

'Well, I think I should borrow a car to take you for a spin and get you out of Sister's way.'

Poppy smiled. She'd never been for a 'spin' before. It was the sort of thing that affluent couples did: went for a spin into the country, to the seaside or for a picnic. She shook her head, however. 'That's very kind, but as Sister never fails to remind us, nursing staff are not allowed to dally with the doctors.' She thought a moment then added, 'Or the patients, or the locals, or anyone really. We're either on duty, or have to stay in our rooms and darn our stockings.'

Michael Archer raised his eyebrows. 'British nurses must not stray from the path of righteousness!'

'Certainly not,' Poppy said. 'What about British doctors?'

'Doctors,' he said, 'are allowed a little more leeway.' He touched Poppy's arm lightly. 'I go now in search of eggs! I'll call in and see you one day. Ward 5, wasn't it?'

'Please don't!' Poppy said in alarm. 'Sister Shrew will have hysterics.'

But he just winked at her and went on down the street with his canvas bag.

Chapter Seven

My dear Poppy,
I was so proud to receive your letter and to hear that
you'd decided to nurse in France. I am sending this letter
care of Devonshire House and I'm sure it will find you.

I have been feeling rather low lately, but your news
gave me such a boost. If you were here, I expect you
would ask me why I was feeling low and I think I would
probably answer that it's because I haven't got a lot to
do. We've been more or less promised that women will
be granted the vote (heaven be praised!) when this
damnable war ends, so it doesn't seem worthwhile

expending energy on that particular fight, which is almost won.

My other occupation, the giving out of white feathers, has also come to a halt. You will know that conscription has started so that a great deal more men are now going off to fight, but I've begun to wonder (I'm going to be perfectly honest here) if I ever should have demanded that other women's sons sacrifice their lives when I have no sons of my own to lose.

I will tell you about something which happened to me which is much on my mind. Some months back, I approached two young men at a charity function. They were brothers and both said they were in reserved occupations – one a carpenter, the other a glazier. Knowing that they hadn't volunteered to fight, I spoke to them sternly for some minutes, asking if they thought it was right that other young men of their own age should be in the trenches in appalling conditions, while they stayed at home in safety. Finding out their address, the next day I sent them each a white feather.

This was about eight months ago and I didn't think much more about it, but just two weeks back I was woken early in the morning by a woman hammering at my door. It was the mother of these two boys, quite hysterical, telling me that one son had been hit by a mortar and no trace of him remained, the other had his arms blown off by a grenade and died of trauma and blood loss. On the same day!

It was a terrible shock for me, but, of course, nothing compared to how it was for that poor woman. She was *accompanied by her sister, who had to interpose herself between us, or I believe the bereaved woman would have actually attacked me.*

Since then I've been thinking very deeply about the giving out of feathers and have decided not to continue. I still think everyone ought to fight for their country and defend what is theirs, but they must decide this for themselves.

I am taking a back seat and joining a comforts group – yes, one of those enclaves of upper-class women I so despised! Perhaps you will find an assortment of knitted scarves on their way to you very soon. Please don't worry about writing often – I know how busy you must be and the important thing is caring for the men, our brave soldiers.

Yours with affection,

Enid Luttrell

Receiving this letter, Poppy got one of the postcards she'd bought and, deciding not to mention either white feathers or her troubles with Sister, gave Miss Luttrell her new address at the hospital and said that things were going well for her in France. She added a PS to ask that, if possible, the comforts group might knit some warm bedsocks for the boys in her ward, for those who were immobile – particularly those with only one leg – tended to suffer terribly with aches and cold in the limb which remained.

*

The doctors and consultants did a round of the hospital wards every day, usually after dinner and before the boys had their afternoon nap. This meant all the patients had to be fed, watered and tidied by one o'clock, leaving no trace of trays, bowls or food debris to sully the pristine condition of the ward and bring down the wrath of Sister Shrew. On the arrival of the medical officers, Sister would glide down the centre of the ward (like a luxury liner, Poppy wrote to tell Matthews) accompanied by a nurse on each side, with a convoy of doctors bringing up the rear.

While this little ceremony was going on, Poppy and the other VADs and orderlies would be occupied doing some tidy job out of the way of the main action, writing a letter home for a man who didn't have use of his arms, or helping two or three 'up patients' with a jigsaw. If it happened that the doctors arrived when Sister was occupied with a dying man or a patient's family had arrived to speak to her, one of the nurses would take her place at the head of the procession and, excitingly, a VAD would be asked to join the doctors' round.

So far, this VAD had not been Poppy, but she watched closely how things worked in the hopes that one day, by some twist of fate, it might be her turn to be chosen. The medical officers – two, three or four of them – approached each patient in turn, looked at their charts, studied movement in their remaining limbs and queried

61

various bodily functions. Following this, after consulting each other and sometimes Sister, they decided what should happen next to that patient. He might have to lose another slice of a limb that had turned gangrenous and was not healing, or have to start a different treatment. He might be found fit enough to return to his regiment or – the golden prize – be told he could join the next group going back to Blighty. This lucky man could be picked out by the blue label tied to his bed-frame and the broad smile on his face.

Poppy soon realised that the doctors differed as to how strict or how lenient they were and this affected what course of action they recommended. Some felt that a certain patient had suffered enough and were all for giving him a ticket home. Others believed that the only purpose of a hospital was to get a man well enough to return to fight. On one doctors' round she heard a surgeon insist quite forcefully that the army could certainly find a one-armed man something useful to do in Flanders, and saw the face of that same man (who had certainly thought he was going home) turn pale with shock.

'What on earth are these?' Sister Sherwood exclaimed, studying the coloured bundles which turned up in a parcel from England some two weeks after Poppy's request to Miss Luttrell.

'They're bedsocks, Sister,' Poppy replied.

'And why have I got them?'

'Well, some of the men mentioned to me that their feet were cold, and in Netley we used to have bedsocks for them and I thought one of the comforts groups could –'

'Oh, in Netley!' said Sister. 'That would be the Netley, of course, where the sky is blue and the sun always shines.'

The two other VADs smirked at this, but Poppy stared straight ahead of her and said nothing. When she'd first arrived she thought she probably had spoken a bit too much about Netley – about how the patients were always playing tricks on the nurses, about how nice they looked in their blue hospital-issue suits, about their singing of marching songs to accompany the gramophone while their bandages were being changed – but she'd only been making conversation. When she'd realised that every time she mentioned Netley, Sister took it as a direct slight, she'd stopped.

There was a silence, then Poppy said, 'May I give them to anyone who asks for them?'

Sister tutted. 'They're very gaudy, aren't they? They look as if the women who knitted them used whatever old scraps of wool were left at the bottom of their baskets.'

'Yes, Sister,' Poppy said.

'But,' she said grudgingly, 'I suppose so.'

'Thank you, Sister.'

*

At doctors' round two days later, the ward was just as tidy, but all the patients with only one leg, whether in traction or not, sported a loosely knitted bedsock in red, pink, green or blue – or a combination of all these colours for, as Sister had suspected, wool was getting scarce and the women had indeed used whatever lengths they could find.

There were four senior doctors on this particular round, and Sister Shrew headed the tour as usual. Poppy, playing a game of dominoes with Corporal Tanner, listened to what was being said and heard that the ward was going to be cleared as much as possible because fresh casualties were coming in from Ypres – usually called 'Wipers' by the boys – a town often under attack because of its valuable position on the front line. This meant that six patients from Ward 5, all of whom had recovered well from their most recent operations, were to be given Blighty tickets. The group included Private Norman with his leg and two arms in splints, and five others with plastered-up legs still in traction.

'Lucky blighters!' came the call as soon as the doctors had left the ward.

'Goin' home, goin' home, goin' home!' came the triumphant chant from those given a blue ticket.

'Go and see my wife, will you?' someone called. 'Let her know I'm all right.'

'You give me your address and I'll do more than see her!' came the reply.

'Did you have to sleep with Sister to get that Blighty ticket?' another asked, and that joke ran around the ward, but quietly because although Sister had stepped outside to speak to one of the doctors, her presence could still very much be felt.

'I'm going to hop straight along to the limb place to demand a new leg and two new arms,' Private Norman said.

'D'you think you'll get all three at once?' someone asked. 'Or is it like rationing – you get one thing and then have to go to the back of the queue again for the next?'

The ragging went on, with those going home promising to keep in touch with those who weren't, and young Private Ridge offered to visit anyone's girlfriend in England and give them a good time. This led to someone saying that if Ridgey went anywhere near his girlfriend then Ridgey would end up with his other leg chopped off, so Poppy quickly stepped in to change the mood, suggesting that they all did one of the quizzes in an old *Photoplay* magazine on the table.

Guessing that at least one or two of these boys with limb injuries might end up in Netley for the rest of their treatment, Poppy longed to write a 'wish you were here' message to Moffat and Gallagher on the fresh white plaster of their legs, but under the watchful eye of Sister, she did not dare.

That afternoon, the departing men's medical notes were tidied into files to be despatched with them, their personal possessions and any souvenirs of battle packed into their kitbags, and postcards sent to their families to tell them what was happening. Spaces being available on a hospital ship bound for Southampton that evening, a dozen orderlies appeared, ready to wheel the boys' beds on to the backs of lorries with as little bumping as possible and drive them the short distance to the docks.

Off they went to envious cheers and several choruses of 'Goodbyeee'. Poppy's last glimpse of Private Norman was of his big stripy bedsock, dangling from his leg like a flag, disappearing around the corner. Seeing him go, her eyes stung with sudden tears. She'd very much liked him and the way he always made light of his injuries. How much of it was just bravado in front of the others, though? How would he be able to manage at home? What place was there in England for a man with three limbs missing?

She sighed. This was a rotten, stinking war, whatever side you were on.

Ward 5,
Casino Hospital,
Nr Boulogne-sur-Mer,
France

20ᵗʰ March 1916

Dear Matthews,
I can hardly bear to put this in writing. I last wrote to you about the newspaper cutting with Freddie and his

new bride. Well, something terrible has happened which has put everything into perspective, so that any matters of the heart seem of little consequence.

A couple of days ago at doctors' round, six boys were told they would be going back to Blighty to make room for some new casualties. There was the usual fuss in the ward – the teasing and the singing and so on. After that a solemn quietness descended on all of them and a sadness, too, for some of them had been serving in the same regiment and had become like brothers. They must have been wondering if they'd ever see each other again. The staff were very quiet, too, because we all have our favourites and Private Norman – he with three missing limbs – had become one of mine (although I would never let anyone else know this, as Sister Shrew has a down on us having favourites).

When they were wheeled off by the orderlies in the late afternoon, each chap was wearing a new warm bedsock on his foot (kindly sent by Miss Luttrell's comforts group) and those of us who could get to the window waved as they were wheeled on to the back of a Red Cross open lorry. I remember saying to one of the other VADs that it wasn't far to Boulogne docks and thank goodness it had stopped raining, which, in the circumstances, was the most inconsequential remark in the world.

Anyway, when my shift ended I went downstairs to the nurses' quarters, only to find that orderlies had cleared a whole new section of the basement and were putting up bedsteads in readiness for the arrival of more nurses. I decided to keep out of their way so I went to the canteen and was sitting with some soup when an orderly ran in shouting that a hospital ship had been torpedoed halfway across the Channel and gone down with all hands.

Everyone got in a frightful stew and started rushing about trying to find out which ship it was. It turned out to be the ship (I won't name it, because of the censor) that had left with not only our six boys but dozens of recovering soldiers from different wards who'd been given a Blighty ticket. Boys not just from here, but also from other nearby hospitals.

Everyone was speechless and horrified. There were lots of tears, even from hardbitten orderlies. It was the most heartbreaking thing to think that we've patched up these boys, removed their shrapnel, treated their wounds, plastered their broken limbs, and fed and nurtured them, and all for nothing.

We got to bed very late, for everyone was waiting for more news to come in. We were all so angry about it being a hospital ship (marked, of course, with a big red cross on each side) that some were saying that, to get our own back, we should refuse to look after the wounded German prisoners of war. There were many more of us who didn't think this was right, however, and later there came intelligence to say that it was not a torpedo or a U-boat which had sunk our ship, but a mine. And mines *can't tell the difference between a hospital ship and one carrying troops, of course.*

This morning our ward had something else to bear, for we discovered that about half the casualties on the hospital ship had been rescued by nearby craft, but none of these were Ward 5 boys. This was because, their legs or arms still being in traction, they were secured to their beds with wooden 'scaffolding'. In the water, naturally the wood had floated, and in the process had turned the patients upside down and drowned them. Matron-in-Charge has now decreed that no more men should be sent home in traction.

And now I can't stop thinking about the last moments of those boys. They went off with their bedsocks on and there's a picture in my head of a vast expanse of grey sea, with two or three coloured bedsocks floating upon it, so tiny that they can hardly be seen. I feel very sad as it seems more than tragic that they should be drowned when they'd overcome so much and were almost back home. Better they should have died in the trenches than have their lives snatched away again like this. It feels as if they've died twice.

Oh, do think about coming out here, Matthews! I need someone to talk to and I promise not to go on about Freddie de Vere. Look, I've hardly mentioned him in this letter!

With my love,

Poppy (or Pearson, if you like) xxx

Chapter Eight

Poppy found the next couple of weeks hard to get through, for everyone was subdued – or, worse, snappy. Sister was more shrewish than ever, finding fault with Poppy's bedmaking and her laying up of trays ('Sometimes I feel you have completely the wrong attitude to be a VAD') and saying she lacked professionalism because she caught her laughing at a patient's joke. Poppy even got ticked off for leaving a pillow with its open end facing the door, because one of Sister's rules was that pillows should all show the same smooth side ('to look tidier when the doctors come into the ward').

Seemingly just to spite her, Sister found Poppy urgent things to do when it was time for her dinner break and managed to organise the rota so that she didn't get a half-day off for three weeks.

Should she go to Matron and ask to be moved? Such a complaint would be frowned on, Poppy knew, because it sounded so petty and childish to say that your superior was picking on you when, all around you, boys were fighting for their lives. Besides, although the tasks she was allowed to carry out appeared to be insignificant, at least she was doing something. She fumed inside, though, knowing that this wasn't what she'd come to France to do. She'd wanted to make a difference to the lives of those who were injured, not to count the number of sheets in the linen press – the orderlies could do that well enough.

In Netley, Poppy had had a few not too badly injured patients she liked to think were her particular responsibility. She changed their dressings, wrote their letters and generally kept a special eye on them. There was no chance, however, of her or anyone else having the same sort of relationship with any boys in Ward 5.

One day, Sister had a painful hand infection and was especially irritable and difficult, criticising everything Poppy did and even finding fault with the manner in which she'd sprinkled boracic powder on a man's grazed back. By the time Poppy had finished her shift and the night staff came on, she was looking forward to being alone and having a weep. She wondered again about going to Matron, but suppose Matron told Sister that Poppy had complained about her? Wouldn't things just be worse than ever? What should she do? Had she made a terrible mistake in coming to France?

Going downstairs to her cubicle, she found that even a moment alone was going to be denied her, because two girls in nurse's uniform were perched on crates in the communal part of the basement, the 'lounge' that no one ever had time to lounge in.

'Hi!' they chorused.

The one nearest to her said in a broad accent, 'How're you doing?'

'I'm doing very well, thank you,' said Poppy, and the two girls burst out laughing.

'Oh, do excuse us!' said the first girl, who had light gingery hair in rather extravagant waves. 'It's just that it's been drummed into us that English girls are really polite and well mannered, and you replied in exactly the way we thought you would.'

'Well, I'm glad to hear it,' said Poppy, for both girls were beaming at her and there was absolutely no way she could have taken offence. She introduced herself.

The girls said they were American nurses and their names were Dorothy Manning and Matilda Butt, usually called Dot and Tilly, which prompted Poppy to say they sounded like a singing duo.

'We can do that, too!' Tilly said. She had the shortest hair Poppy had seen on a young woman, and (certainly forbidden in Poppy's ward) a pair of small, sparkling earrings.

'In fact, we're from Chicago and there's not much we can't do!' said her friend.

'But why are you here when America isn't in the war?' Poppy asked. 'Although we're very pleased to have you, I'm sure,' she added hastily.

'We're volunteers,' Dot said. 'There's a whole parcel of us – doctors and nurses – who've come over to lend a hand. I don't think it'll be long before we're all in the war together, though.'

'Do you know what ward you'll be working on?' Poppy asked, crossing her fingers it would be Ward 5.

They shook their heads.

'We're not working in this hospital,' Tilly said. 'We're at the place that used to be the Savoy, down the road. It's just that they've run out of staff quarters there.'

'Not to mention the fact that the doctors have already grabbed all the best rooms,' put in Dot. 'The end result is, they've billeted us here. We're just waiting for our beds to be put up and our lockers to arrive, then we're going to unpack and go into town for something to eat.'

'There's a canteen here,' Poppy offered.

Both girls gave her raised-eyebrow looks.

'We're not that desperate – not yet,' said Dot. 'Come out to supper with us, won't you? You can tell us the best places to eat.'

Poppy shook her head. 'I doubt if I could do that. I've not been here long myself and I certainly don't know anywhere to go.'

'Then just come anyway.'

Poppy thought for a moment. Should she stay in the basement on her own and have a cry, or go out with two girls called Dot and Tilly who looked like movie stars?

'That would be grand,' she said.

In the little restaurant they found, Poppy felt a bit shy at first, because the American girls were well travelled and seemed much more sophisticated, but they also giggled a lot, were great fans of Mary Pickford and knew all the latest movie news, so it didn't take long before the three of them were gossiping like old friends.

The next day brought a letter from Billy.

8903 D Company

Dear Sis,

Well here i am back on the front. Well not quite on the front but certainly close so i hear the bloody guns firing all nite loud enough to make a bloke want to scream at the blighters to shut up. I wish i could of stayed at the farm in Scotland – i would have been quite happy up there and clear of the war but no. Some busybody thought it would be a good idea to get me back to France. I won't say where i am because of the censor but i think it is south from where you are in Bulloyne (i am not sure how you spell it).

My foot is completely healed now and i won't talk about the reasons i am here as i don't want everyone knowing my business, so i am glad i am in a different regiment. The best thing is they have asked for volunteers to be stretcher bearers wen we move up the line and i have put my name down so it means i do not have to go out and be a target for Fritz as we will only be sent out when firing has stopped.

We have a dog here – it runs between groups of lads passing on messages. Sometimes if there is not much going on we have a laugh. We send him off with pictures (that is cartoons a matey has drawn) of the field marshal in the bog and whoever gets them has to send them off quick to the next group before an officer sees them.

I think i am managing better this time tho it is still hell on earth. I took a lad to a bandaging station in the middle of the night as he had woke to find a rat nawing at his hand (it was as big as a cat he said) and before he could kill it, it had bit his finger of. I think he would of bled to death if it hadn't been for me. He said he was so deep asleep and dreaming of home that he did not want to wake up.

Have you heard from ma? I would like to no she's alright. i sent her a field postcard when i was on the farm but have not herd anything since.

Let me no what it's like there.
Love from your brother Billy.

Poppy, pleased to receive this, wrote back on another postcard to say that the last she'd heard, Ma and the girls were fine. She added a plea to Billy to keep his head down and not do anything silly, but just remember how lucky he was, saying (as enigmatically as possible) that no one would be able to help him if the sort of thing which happened before happened again. After thinking that even this might be too much information on an open postcard, she put it in an envelope before sending it.

*

A week went by and Sister's hand got worse. Apparently – so Poppy heard from the other nurses – it had started with a small cut between thumb and forefinger, which had quickly become infected by something passed on by a patient who'd been in the trenches. Nurses were supposed to wear rubber gloves when bandaging or treating casualties, but the stocks of these had run very low – and the demand for them in operating theatres was so high – that they weren't always available. Sister's hand had now puffed up so much that she could no longer move it and she had it in a sling. This meant, of course, that she couldn't undertake some of her usual duties, which left her more time to supervise – and criticise – Poppy and anyone else she currently had a down on. During the week, many an orderly was castigated or told in no uncertain terms that his work wasn't good enough. Even the two other VADs were chastised for, firstly, taking too long over dinner in the canteen, and secondly and much more seriously, allowing crumbs to fall into a patient's bed and be noticed by one of the doctors.

'The absolute rotter!' Dot said to Poppy on hearing the full story of Freddie de Vere. 'So, he actually went and married someone else?'

'He did. I mean, he hadn't proposed to me or anything, but I was felt that he just might, when the war was over. And he did assure me that there was absolutely nothing between him and Miss Cardew.'

It was early evening and the two girls were in the basement, waiting for Tilly to appear before going out for something to eat. Life, Poppy had discovered, was much more bearable now that the two American nurses were around.

'So,' Dot said, her eyes big and round, 'if you'd married him you would have ended up Lady of the Manor.'

Poppy smiled sadly. 'Yes, can you believe it!' She couldn't help remembering her brief encounter with Freddie in the moonlit garden of Airey House and the way, the next morning, he'd referred to her as the beautiful lady of the lake. She'd believed it then, all right . . .

'Did you ever see Miss Cardew?' Dot asked eagerly. 'Is she a real swell?'

Poppy nodded. 'I've seen her many times. Her family used to visit the de Veres for shooting parties and afternoon tea and so on.'

'Golly!'

'They're very well-to-do. She was a debutante.'

'I'm not sure what that is but it sounds real impressive. Kinda like being titled, is it?'

'Something like that,' Poppy said. She slid off the bed. 'I've got a photograph of them, a wedding photograph, if you'd like to . . .'

'Oh, sure I would!'

Poppy got out the medical dictionary and found the cutting. 'I wasn't going to look at this again – not until

I felt I was over him, and then I was going to throw it away.'

'Nooo!' Dot said. 'You must keep it for ever, and then when you're old you'll be able to remember him fondly and know that he was just a stepping stone before meeting the great love of your life.'

Poppy, smiling at this, handed over the cutting and Dot stared at it for some moments.

'Yeah. I see why you fell for him – he's quite a looker,' she said. 'And her, the new wifey, looks like a real lady.'

'I know. They're terribly well suited. Cook used to say that their relationship was just about money and a contract for houses and land, but I'm not so sure.'

'Gee,' said Dot, still gazing at the newspaper photograph. 'It's kinda like a movie.'

'Phew! What a day!' Tilly had come in while they'd been staring at the cutting and was now looking over their shoulders.

'You've missed a great story!' Dot exclaimed. She glanced at Poppy. 'That is, a great but tragic story.'

'Hey, who's the bridegroom?' Tilly said, jabbing a finger at the picture of Freddie. 'Looks like Wallace Reid the movie star.'

Dot nudged her. 'But he's a rotter! A screwed-down stinking rotter.'

Tilly gave a squeak of surprise, then said, 'Well, of course. You can see it, can't you, just by looking at him.'

Wallace Reid, Poppy thought. She would buy *Movie Star Magazine* and see if Freddie really did look like him.

She waited for Tilly to finish studying the cutting, then folded it carefully and put it back in the book. She wasn't ready to throw it away just yet.

Dot turned to Tilly. 'Where have you been all this time? I finished an hour ago.'

'I haven't finished,' Tilly said. 'And nor have you, actually. A score of ambulances has brought some casualties from Ypres and as many nurses as possible are wanted on duty.'

Dot groaned. 'I'm starving and tired and have chilblains.'

'You're lucky to have toes to have chilblains on,' Tilly said briskly, flapping her apron. 'Come on, our patients are waiting.' She waved farewell to Poppy. 'See you later, maybe?'

Poppy, disappointed not to be going out, was thinking she might go to the canteen on her own when one of the other VADs from her ward appeared. 'You're wanted!' she said. 'All hands on deck.'

'New boys coming in?' Poppy asked, but the VAD had already run back up the stairs.

Poppy followed her. It used to be both thrilling and terrifying when new casualties arrived at Netley, but it was different here. The injuries were worse – bloodier, gorier, the men filthier with mud and running with lice – but she wasn't allowed to do anything really useful. Mentally she prepared herself for an evening of standing about handing bandages to the nurses and filling up water jugs.

Chapter Nine

Going back to Ward 5, Poppy found that there were five nurses and three VADs ready to take care of the new boys. But no Sister Shrew, she realised, and remembered that she'd gone off at dinner time and not been seen since.

'Has Sister been told we've got new men coming in?' Poppy whispered to one of the nurses.

The nurse shook her head. 'Poor Sister's got a fever from the infection in her hand and her arm has swelled up like a balloon. I think she'll be off for the rest of the week.'

'Oh, really?' Poppy tried to sound sincere. 'What rotten news.'

Matron arrived with a new sister who was going to take charge of the ward in the Shrew's absence. Poppy had seen her in the hospital canteen – not to speak to, of course, because high-ranking staff were apt to distance themselves from VADs – but coming and going in a busy, important way. An attractive woman in her thirties, Sister Gradley introduced herself and said that she'd be staying until Sister Sherwood was fit enough to return.

Poppy, looking at her, tried to judge what she'd be like and whether or not she approved of VADs. Oh, just let her be more reasonable, more open, nicer than Sister Shrew . . .

There were seven new casualties coming into Ward 5, four with stomach wounds, two with broken bones and multiple shrapnel wounds, and one who'd been gassed as well as having other injuries. They'd received these injuries two or three days before, but had been stuck in no-man's-land, where it had proved almost impossible to reach them. As a result of this time delay, many of their wounds had turned gangrenous.

Waiting to be cleaned up, they were lying on waterproof-covered mattresses placed together in a section partitioned off from the main ward by screens on wheels.

'They were too weak to climb out of the trenches on their own, and in any case they were very close to the German line,' one of the ambulance men told the Ward 5 nurses. 'We waited and waited, and in the end we had to wave a white flag and shout over to Fritz for a truce.'

'Did you get them out easily?' someone asked.

'Not exactly,' he said. 'Two of them were lying in a foot of mud in the bottom of the trench – it was lucky that they weren't face down or they would have drowned. Another had somehow got rolled up in barbed wire and we had to cut him out.' The ambulance man shook his head. 'There were a few more of our chaps lying about, but by the time we got to them they were already dead.' He added chillingly, 'Very much dead.'

There was a silence, then one of the VADs asked, 'So the Germans did allow a truce in the end?'

'Yeah, because Jerry had wounded to bring in, too,' said a second ambulance man. 'Both sides stopped firing for ten minutes and everyone scrambled around in the mud until they'd got their own boys back.'

'These chaps have only had a quick once-over by a doctor – there was no time for anything else – so you may find other injuries no one has spotted yet,' said the first man, wheeling back a screen.

As one, the staff turned their attention to the sight now before them: seven dreadfully injured men, caked in mud and blood and in as bad a condition as any casualty Poppy had ever seen before. Unreachable for too long, buffeted and jolted by the journey to the hospital, occasionally a groan or great sigh would come from one of them. Mostly, though, they were silent. *Did they know they'd been rescued?* Poppy wondered. *Did they know where they were, or even that they were alive?*

Once the ambulance men had gone, Sister Gradley counted up the assembled staff. 'We are nine altogether. I suggest one of the qualified nurses keeps an eye on those boys who are more or less settled down for the night, and the rest of us take an injured man each.' She nodded towards the two older VADs. 'You've been out here a while so you know the ropes, and . . .' she looked at Poppy appraisingly, 'our young VAD here can work with me.'

Poppy smiled and nodded. Even though it was a huge responsibility, it would be too terrible to be the only person on the ward not allowed to help with the new boys, to be relegated to making the night-time cocoa.

Sister Gradley proved to be brisk, competent and – much to Poppy's relief – fair. She asked what experience Poppy had had, and being told that at Netley she'd been trusted to do most basic tasks, said she'd allow Poppy to wash and prepare one of the new intake of soldiers ready for inspection by the doctors, as long as Poppy promised to tell her immediately if there was anything she felt she couldn't cope with. Poppy, looking at the casualty she'd been assigned to, said a little prayer that she would be able to cope, and also that he wouldn't die while she was looking after him.

The soldier – her soldier – was a tall, thin, young man with muddy, slicked-back hair and a deep gash on his cheek through which his jaw could be seen. He was wearing khaki, but any stripes or regimental badges had disappeared under layers of mud and caked-on blood. One of his arms was crushed and hanging, misshapen, off the bed, and his boots and puttees were so filthy that it was difficult to say what they were covered with. His eyes were closed and at that moment there was no indication as to whether he was conscious or not.

'You'll have to cut his uniform off,' the nurse next to her said. 'And his boots, probably.'

Poppy nodded and, rather nervous now, went to the head of the bed. She knew she had to reassure her patient, tell him where he was, and she felt around his neck to see if he had a name tag. *Pte Terry Ian Burroughs*, it said, and underneath someone had scratched, *Tibs*.

Very well, Poppy thought. She would call him Tibs for now, and when he got better she would call him by his proper name. Right then, though, she knew he needed to be made to feel comfortable and safe.

'Tibs?' she said. 'Hello, Tibs. Do you know where you are?'

There was a long pause and his eyelids flickered. 'Hell?' came the hoarse reply.

Poppy took his good hand in hers and held it tightly. 'No, they've brought you to Boulogne. You're in what they call the Casino Hospital. My name's Pearson. I'm a VAD.'

'Ah.' He breathed in deeply and groaned. 'On a clear day you can see Blighty,' he said, speaking, as much as was possible, without moving the gashed side of his face.

'I believe you can,' Poppy replied, for that was what the boys said, though she thought it was just wishful thinking on their part.

'I remember being carried out of the trench . . .' he muttered, then his voice slurred, his head dropped to one side and his body slumped.

Either he was sleeping, Poppy thought, or he'd lapsed into unconsciousness. She could only tell he was still alive because of his hoarse breathing.

'First of all, I'm going to get you out of that uniform,' she said. She'd been told to always explain what she was doing to a patient, even if he seemed to be unconscious. Besides, she found that she was strangely reassured by the sound of her own voice speaking so rationally and calmly, as if she was confident about what she was doing. 'It's going to be difficult cutting through this tough uniform, but it's better off than on, and the doctors have to see what they're dealing with.'

With heavy scissors Poppy cut through the thick khaki material, removed some things from an inside pocket of his army jacket and put them into his locker.

'There's your wallet going in your locker,' she said, 'and some letters and a photograph of a very pretty girl sitting on a farm gate. They'll all be quite safe here.'

She peeled off the front of the jacket and tried to ease out his right arm. He woke and started to shout almost immediately, grabbing her hand with his own good one and begging her to stop, to leave him alone.

'I can't do that,' she said. 'It's what we have to do – get you ready for the doctors to see you so they can decide what treatment you need. I have to do it,' she repeated. 'I'm so sorry if it's painful.'

She slit the sleeve of his jacket right up to the armpit and then lifted the material off, trying not to wrinkle her nose at the strong smell of sweat. Slowly, carefully, she began to unwind the sodden bandage around his shoulder that had been put on by someone at a bandaging station. She thought that, very probably, one of his wounds had got infected, for there was no mistaking the foul stink of gangrene. By now, he had passed out again.

Taking off the last twist of bandage, the wound where his arm met his shoulder was exposed and Poppy was relieved to see that, although quite serious, it was by no means the worst injury she'd ever seen. There were lice and fleas on him, too, which had crawled out from the seams of his uniform and were now dropping on the floor around them. There was nothing she could do about these, however, apart from tread on as many as she could.

Working quickly, she dropped the jacket pieces on the floor and cut off the two vests he wore, trying to breathe in a shallow way. She knew that sometimes, if a man had lost his kit or become separated from his platoon, it meant he had to stay in the same clothes, socks and boots for two or even three weeks. Six weeks was the most she'd heard of – and she didn't want to hazard a guess about the things Tibs was wearing.

'Now I'm going to start cleaning you up,' she said. 'And, Tibs, it looks as though you really need it.'

She sponged the top half of him as carefully as possible, coming and going to the little kitchen and getting fresh water then dabbing him dry. This done, she laid a blanket over his top half to keep him warm. Alongside her, the other nurses and VADs were doing the same with various degrees of difficulty. One of the new boys clearly didn't know where he was because he was shouting at the top of his voice, 'Help! Leave me alone! Get your hands off me!' Another was crying with pain and trying to curl into a ball, which was making his nurse's job very hard.

The bottom half of Tibs looked like it would be more problematic, but the trousers weren't going to come off until his boots and filthy, stinking puttees which wound around his calves were removed, so she decided to tackle these first. His feet were stuck hard inside his boots, so one of the other nurses had to give her some cutters, which enabled her to slit down the front of the boot and ease his foot out that way. This she did.

As she began to unwind the filthy, clammy fabric of the puttees, the stench that hit her was so ghastly that she knew some of his flesh must have gone gangrenous. She walked to the window, took a deep breath and then returned to her patient.

'Not much longer, Tibs,' she said, trying to sound as if this wasn't the most dreadful task she'd ever under-taken in all her life. 'Just your socks to go.'

Carefully, gently, she began to roll his sock down, exposing his ankle and foot, which was sodden, pale and flabby, like the flesh of a dead fish. Trench foot, she thought. She'd seen it before, but never so bad as this. She started to peel away his sock from his foot in order to expose his toes and found two of these were black. Not black with dirt, but black because they were dead. The thick sock he'd been wearing had somehow embedded itself in the flesh of his foot and she had to cut and gently prise out the sock's fibres from his toes as well as she could. As she took off the last bits of the sock, however, a toe came with it, completely rotted away.

Poppy dropped the toe on to a metal tray together with the sodden scraps of material and, feeling herself swaying, held on to the head of the bed. She put the surgical scissors down on the locker and managed to get to the window, where she held on to the sill to keep herself upright. She breathed deeply.

Sister Gradley, seeing her gulping air, came over. 'Difficult one?' she asked.

'Just a little,' Poppy said, her voice shaky. 'Bad shoulder wound, trench foot and gangrene. Loss of at least one toe.'

'You've done very well so far,' said Sister Gradley, 'but do you want me to help you now?'

Poppy was reluctant to say that she couldn't manage, but, moved by Sister's kind concern and the dread of what might be found when the second boot was removed, said, 'Yes, please. Perhaps you could help me get his other boot and puttee off?'

'Of course.'

Fifteen minutes later, Tibs was washed and pyjama-ed, and Sister had moved on to help someone else. When exposed, the flesh on his other foot had been white and dead-looking, and his toes grey, but at least they'd still been attached to his foot, so Sister thought there was a good chance that most of them could be saved. The covering had now been removed from the mattress and Tibs's bed had been made up around him, with a cage at the foot preventing the bedclothes from touching his toes. He'd been given drugs to ease the pain and had fallen into a deep sleep. The doctors not being expected imminently, Sister pulled the screens around Tibs's bed and told Poppy to go and get some sleep herself.

Poppy found, however, that although immensely tired, she was strangely reluctant to leave the ward. Tibs seemed completely out of it, but she squeezed his good hand, said she hoped he'd have a reasonable night and that she'd see him in the morning. Looking at him, so pale, with his poor injured feet, his gashed cheek and the wound in his shoulder, she felt an overwhelming surge of tenderness for him, even though they hadn't exchanged more than a few words. She wondered if his mother or sweetheart (the girl on the gate?) were waiting at home for news of him. Had they already heard he was missing? Were they, fearing that telegram, becoming alarmed at every knock on the door?

It was two o'clock in the morning and she had to be on duty in just over five hours. Suddenly feeling she had to lie down or she'd keel over, Poppy went to her bed.

Chapter Ten

As it turned out, Poppy was awake by five o'clock in the morning and found it impossible to get back to sleep, anxiously wondering how Tibs was and if anything terrible had happened to him overnight. Might she have missed something vital? A shard of glass, a piece of shrapnel?

Trying not to wake her fellow nurses, she washed in the little bathroom, then went into the canteen and helped herself to a breakfast of two small fried eggs on toast.

She found an English newspaper, only a week old, which concentrated mostly on the battles and skirmishes that the Allies had won, but carefully omitted to say at what cost they had been achieved. The newspaper was strident in its praise of the generals in charge and informed the public that Britain was gaining land and definitely moving towards victory. All very gung-ho, Poppy thought, but not exactly the story they were hearing from the boys who were just back from the front. There were no photographs of British casualties, of course, in case it should affect morale, so the only dead soldiers anyone ever saw in newspaper pictures were German ones.

The paper contained recipes for making soup from potato peelings and several features urging its readers to make do and mend, but, extraordinarily, the centre pages were given over to photographs of a big charity party in a candlelit ballroom in London. Here, there seemed to be no war. Here, ladies in shiny, sparkling gowns were being swirled around the dance floor by gentlemen in evening dress. The bill of fare was given: lobster and fillet steak, followed by rare, out-of-season fruits. The party, it declared, had been held in aid of the war effort, but – eating her extremely small eggs and knowing of the shortages at home – Poppy wondered why it had needed to be quite so lavish. Couldn't everyone just have stayed at home and sent the money instead? How did all those who were eating potato-peel soup and unravelling their jumpers to knit balaclavas for soldiers react on seeing such extravagance? She sniffed disapprovingly over the photographs, then studied each one to make sure none showed Freddie and the new Mrs de Vere.

Going into Ward 5 at the beginning of her shift, she found Sister Gradley wasn't yet in, but two of the nurses were deep in conversation with a white-gowned doctor. Not wanting to interrupt and anxious to know how Tibs was, Poppy slipped behind one of the screens and tiptoed towards where she'd left him.

He was still there, and he'd clearly been operated on, but he looked uncomfortable and awkward. The gash in his cheek was neatly stitched, his arm – newly bandaged, but already showing blood – was out at an angle, and his poor white feet with blackened toes were covered with a square of cloth.

'Tibs,' Poppy whispered. 'How are you feeling?'

Tibs's eyelids opened and he looked at Poppy.

'You came into this hospital last night,' she explained. 'The ambulance brought you over from a clearing station. I got you ready for the doctors, cut you out of your boots. You may not remember – you seemed to be unconscious for most of the time.'

'You're the VAD?' he asked in a hoarse whisper.

'That's right!' said Poppy.

'How many toes have I lost?'

Poppy thought of the toe that had come off with his sock and pulled a sympathetic face. 'I'm afraid you've lost one for sure.'

'Only one?'

'For now, but I don't know what the surgeons will do about the others. Didn't they say anything to you when they examined you?' she asked, for even with her limited medical knowledge it seemed obvious that several of his toes would have to be removed surgically.

'By the time the doctors arrived, I was barely conscious. And then I went straight in for an op, of course.'

Footsteps were heard on the other side of the screen and, to Poppy's great surprise, Michael Archer – the doctor who'd been talking to the two nurses – appeared.

'Nurse Pearson! How nice to see you,' he said pleasantly, as if they were meeting at a social event. He patted Tibs's good shoulder, then raised his eyebrows at Poppy. 'You're Private Burroughs's personal nurse, are you?'

'Well,' Poppy began, rather embarrassed. 'It's just that I looked after him last night when he came in and I kind of feel, you know, responsible.'

'Very commendable,' Michael Archer said. 'And as a matter of fact, I feel responsible, too, because Private Burroughs came through our clearing station.'

'Did I? I don't remember,' Tibs said.

'I'm not surprised. I only had time to give you a quick examination, but my boss asked me to keep track of you. We're going to try out something fairly new on Private Burroughs here, if Sister agrees.'

'On my toes?' Tibs croaked.

'Not your toes – I'm afraid the damage has already been done there. It's your arm that the doctors are concerned about now. We don't want you to lose it.'

'The wound looks quite clear at the moment,' Poppy said.

Michael Archer nodded. 'There's a new treatment which consists of continually irrigating the wound with a spray of disinfectant. It's been found to prevent the infection which can lead to gangrene.'

'Sounds all right. Can I have it?' Tibs asked.

'I certainly hope we can give it to you and several other suitable candidates in this ward. I'm going to speak to Sister about it now.'

Tibs opened his eyes again. 'Last night, when I came in, I know I wasn't a pretty sight.' He nodded towards Poppy. 'She did me all right, though.' He looked towards his feet and grimaced. 'I'm not a pretty sight now, come to think of it.'

'Trench foot isn't pleasant, but remember that it's better to lose a toe than a nose,' Michael Archer said as he left them.

Later, as Poppy collected the breakfast trays, she overheard two of the nurses talking of the new method of irrigating wounds.

'A young doctor came up from one of the clearing stations to tell us all about it,' one was telling another. 'Apparently it's having remarkable results and really cutting down on the number of amputations.'

'Doctor Archer is a really nice chap,' Poppy blurted out. They looked at her in surprise. 'He was at Netley and so was I,' she explained. 'Oh gosh, I was so green. It was my first day and I didn't realise he was a doctor. I thought he was going to faint, so made him sit down and pushed his head between his legs!'

The following morning produced another reminder of Netley: a picture postcard of the hospital with, on the other side, a message from Matthews.

Still at Netley

28th March 1916

Just a line to let you know that I have applied to Devonshire House to work as a VAD in France – and been accepted!

There! I know you'll be pleased. Of course, I don't know where they'll send me, but I'll try very hard to get close to Boulogne and contact you soonest.
Much love,

Matthews

As if this news wasn't good enough, Poppy had Dot and Tilly to cheer up her off-duty hours, and – even better – another week went by and Sister Shrew had not returned. There were rumours that the Shrew was worse and that the infection had spread throughout her body, then they were told that she was being sent to a sisters' hospital in Calais, prior to returning to England. Feeling a little two-faced, Poppy signed a get well card that the boys in the ward had made, writing on it, *Hope you'll soon be feeling better*. It would have been nice to have added, as one of the nurses suggested, *We miss you on Ward 5*, but this would have been an out-and-out lie. She didn't miss her one bit.

Under Sister Gradley, Poppy felt that at last she was doing what she'd come to France to do: nurse. As a bonus, the ward staff were more relaxed and the patients seemed to pick up on this. There were even pranks played by those who were well enough. On 1st April, an orderly came in with a message saying that King George was going to pay a visit to Ward 5, sending the whole place into a fever of tidying and polishing before Sister realised what the date was. No one would have dared do such a thing if Sister Shrew had been in charge on April Fool's Day.

There were many in the ward, of course, who were not well enough to play pranks: boys who not only had wounds that were slow to heal, but had picked up infections and diseases from the vile conditions on the battlefields. Even if they seemed all right in the daytime, some of them had seen too much. They'd wake screaming in the middle of the night or find it near impossible to get to sleep at all because of the visions that afflicted them. One man had witnessed his best friend blown to pieces in front of him; another's pal had died splayed on barbed wire; yet another, his injured legs smashed so he was unable to move, had seen his mate slowly drown at the bottom of a trench filled with filthy water. Poppy and the other nurses knew that, with some of the lads, even if their visible injuries healed, those wounds in their minds might not.

At the end of that week, a young corporal came in, barely conscious, with a ghastly injury to his head and a bullet which had penetrated his lung and couldn't be removed.

'He can't be operated on,' Sister Gradley said. 'I'm afraid he's just been brought in to die.' She looked out of the window and Poppy saw her take several deep breaths, as if trying to keep her feelings under control. 'We can keep him comfortable, that's all, and try to make his last hours reasonably pleasant and pain-free.'

She asked Poppy to get the details of his family so she could write to them, and Poppy looked through his pockets, telling the lad what she was doing and asking his permission as she did so. In his breast pocket she found a field postcard which the boy had addressed to his mother, ready to send. His family were in Scotland, though, so there seemed little chance of them getting to France before he died. The corporal had already filled in the postcard, ticking the box which said he was *in the pink*, but the bullet which had entered his lung had passed right through the card, leaving a clean round hole in the box marked *I have been injured*.

Poppy handed it over to Sister, who, after some thought, sent it on to the boy's family with a letter saying he was near the end, but was pain-free and quite peaceful.

'In years to come they'll be pleased to have that post-card,' she said.

He died that night.

The next morning, Sister, announcing the sad news to her staff, said she couldn't help but be relieved, for with such terrible injuries the corporal would have been severely brain-damaged. Later that morning, she reminded the boys to send their field postcards home.

'Remember, if your people haven't heard that you're safely with us, they may think you're missing.' She looked round at them all. 'I often get letters from worried moth-ers asking if I've got their boys in my ward. I heard about one poor soul who goes to meet every troop train that arrives at Victoria station in London, even though her boy's been missing for a year and is, of course . . .' She spread her hands and didn't have to finish the sentence.

'You've already written home, haven't you?' Poppy asked Tibs.

Tibs nodded. He'd been in the Casino Hospital for two weeks by then and was making reasonable progress. His cheek had been predicted to heal with very little scarring. Two more dead toes had been removed and surgery had tidied up the lesions, although the ulcerated flesh of his feet caused him continual pain and would probably take several months to return to something approaching normal. His right arm, however, was in a better state, and although a long way off being healed, was – mostly thanks to the new irrigation treatment – looking healthy and free of gangrene.

'I've been thinking, though,' he said. 'I've sent a field postcard to my ma telling her I'm here, but I ought to write to my girl.'

'Of course! I'll help you, if you like,' Poppy offered, knowing he would have difficulty with his right arm being out of use. 'Don't doze off after dinner – we'll write when everyone's having their afternoon rest.'

When she turned up with pencil and pad, though, Tibs didn't seem keen to start. He began by asking Poppy not to put the hospital address at the top of the letter because he didn't want his girl to turn up unexpectedly.

'Why ever not?' Poppy said, for quite often wives and families would come across the Channel to see patients, and hostels and hotels had opened specifi-cally for them.

'I don't want her to see me with my feet all dead and my toes missing,' he explained. 'She's a well-brought-up girl. It wouldn't be nice for her.'

'She'll get used to it,' Poppy said cheerfully. 'I'm well brought up and I have.'

Tibs shook his head, his brow furrowed. He was a good-looking lad, Poppy thought, now that his cheek had been stitched, he'd been shaved and had his hair washed and trimmed.

'She won't care about a few missing toes if she loves you,' she added.

'Dainty, my Violet is. Like her name. She likes things just so. Imagine seeing those disgusting things,' he said, indicating his feet, 'sticking out of the bed in the morning.'

'Tibs, she'll just be happy you've been to war and come out the other side!'

'I don't want her to see me,' Tibs said stubbornly. 'I don't want her pity. In fact, I think it's all over between us.'

'Well, if you say so,' Poppy said, 'but I think you're being daft.'

Tibs dictated his letter.

Dear Violet,

I'm in a military hospital recovering from a few bumps and bruises. Soon I hope to be out of this place, and out of the war, for ever.

I'm glad you're enjoying your new job in the factory. It's good for you to have a little spending money. I know you like your pretty clothes.

Violet, I'm sorry for what I have to tell you next, but I've met a French girl and she has been writing to me and visiting me in hospital. We have become quite close and I feel it is only right to ask you to release me from our engagement.

I am very sorry if this news comes as a disappointment, but a smasher like you will not be long in finding

yourself someone new. Please do not think too badly of me.
Yours truly

Poppy wrote exactly what he dictated, even though she paused halfway through and looked at him, frowning.

'Do you want to sign it *Tibs*?' she said when they'd finished. 'Does she call you Tibs and not Terry?'

'Everyone calls me Tibs.'

'Including the French girl?'

'What? Oh, yes. Yes, she does too.'

Poppy looked at him straight. 'She doesn't exist, does she? There is no French girl.'

'How d'you know that?'

'Because if you'd had letters from her, I would have known. And I would have seen anyone who came visiting.'

Tibs gave her a look, a bleak look, then turned away. 'None of your business,' he said gruffly.

'Tibs, you've lied to Violet, haven't you?' Poppy persisted. 'Have you gone off her?'

'No,' he said, and then again, more miserably, 'no, not a bit of it.'

'Then why?'

'Because Violet wouldn't want a freak with one damaged arm and no toes, that's why. She likes going out dancing – she wouldn't want someone who had to hobble around on their stumps.'

'How d'you know that?' Poppy said. She squeezed his hand. 'Things like that aren't for you to decide. You've got to tell her the truth and let her make up her own mind about what she wants to do.'

He shook his head. 'I'm making it up for her. I know I'm going to be a cripple. She'd have to stay working at the munitions factory for the rest of her life to earn enough money to keep me.'

'I'm sure she'd rather do that than lose you! Listen, we had someone here a while back who was a triple amputee.'

Tibs shrugged.

'He never complained, always made the best of things. We got him up and sorted him out. He was on his way to Roehampton to get fitted with new limbs when the ship he was sailing on struck a mine and that was the end of him.'

Tibs shook his head and wouldn't meet her eyes. 'Well, I'm sorry about him, but that's nothing to do with me. Just send her the letter, will you?' he muttered. 'She'll write back and tell me I'm released from our engagement, and that'll be the end of it.'

Poppy sighed, but did as he'd asked.

Before she went off duty that day, Sister Gradley, after asking to have a quiet word with her, said she hoped Poppy wasn't getting too friendly with any of the patients.

'I couldn't help noticing your attentions to Private Burroughs,' she said. 'And weren't you holding his hand?'

'I didn't . . . I mean, I did squeeze his hand, but in sympathy, not because there's anything between us!' Poppy said, rather shocked. 'He has a fiancée at home and he was writing her a very difficult letter.'

'Very well, but do remember that in the circumstances in which we find ourselves, with our patients relying on us for everything, it's all too easy for pity to be mistaken for love.'

Poppy nodded, thinking that although she did feel, in a way, that she loved Tibs – in fact, loved all the boys – it wasn't *that* sort of love. 'I'll take care.'

'I probably wouldn't have said anything to you, but I happen to know that there was a VAD on this ward last year who behaved quite scandalously,' Sister said. 'She got over-friendly with a young lad and then gave him the big heave-ho.' She lowered her voice. 'I'm afraid he took it badly . . . tried to kill himself.'

'Oh, how dreadful!'

'We're all trying to make sure that such a thing doesn't happen again.'

'Of course not,' Poppy said, rather subdued. 'I'll be very careful.'

Chapter Eleven

Casino Hospital,
Nr Boulogne-sur-Mer,
France

21st April 1916

Dearest Ma,

Thank you for your letter. I'm glad to hear that you and the girls and Aunt Ruby are all well. I'm sorry I've only managed to send you a couple of postcards lately, but things are always so hectic here. Hospital life goes on round the clock, patients come in, go out or – of course – sometimes die, whatever time it is. So far I have not had to do night shift, which everyone says is dire.

Things are so much better in Ward 5 since a certain sister went back to Blighty. We now have Sister Gradley in charge and she is perfectly human and allows me and the other VADs to take care of the boys properly and do everything for them, as much as we wish. Sometimes it's more than we wish, but I've got to a stage now where I almost feel that I've seen it all.

Ma, what do you think? The most exciting thing! We've just heard that the Prince of Wales is coming here this afternoon to inspect the hospital, talk to some of the boys and thank the doctors and nurses for their work. I saw a photograph of him the other day in his army uniform and I must say that he is the best looking man that I've ever seen in khaki. Brave, too – apparently as soon as war broke out he wanted to go to France and fight.

I am going now to help shampoo and shine the ward, hang Union Jacks and pin up pictures of the King and Queen – also, my boys with smashed-up legs say I must hang red, white and blue bunting round their leg hoists. We are a little late with all this preparation, because although we heard a rumour about the Prince coming here early this morning, no one believed it. We are always being told that famous people are coming in to boost morale (on April Fool's Day they said it was the King who was coming, and then Charlie Chaplin was supposed to be in the canteen and half the hospital rushed in there to see him), but this time it's really true because Sister showed us the letter.

Your excited daughter,

Poppy xxx

If Poppy was excited, then Dot and Tilly were beside themselves at the thought of a visit by the handsome twenty-two-year-old prince who was not only heir to the British throne, but hugely popular with the people. Luckily, because Dot and Tilly's hospital was closely aligned with the Casino (and because the two girls were nothing but persistent), they'd persuaded their matron to give them permission to be present at the royal visit.

That morning, Poppy, after getting a tip-off from one of the orderlies, had gone into the attic of the building and discovered a trunk containing yards and yards of red, white and blue flag bunting, last used years ago when the casino had first opened. This was brought downstairs, and Poppy and the orderlies draped it around the top of the bed screens and zigzagged it across the ward from one bed to another.

The boys had been issued with clean pyjamas for the occasion, had any beards or moustaches trimmed neatly, and been given haircuts. There were those among them, of course, who wouldn't even know a royal visit was going on, and men who were either in a coma, were seriously ill or had only recently had operations were wheeled into a quiet, screened-off corner of the ward. Tibs, however, was considered well enough to join in the fun, as his cheek was knitting together nicely and the wound in his upper arm was still free of infection. It was just his feet, and more especially his toes, which were causing the doctors some concern. That, and the fact that since he'd got Poppy to write to his fiancée, he'd been quiet and depressed.

When Poppy had finished decorating with the bunting, she took her place by the door of Ward 5. By this time, there were nurses by the beds, nurses on the stairs, nurses on the balcony. There were also doctors, surgeons, orderlies and 'up patients' lining the hallways. Around midday, distant cheers were heard, a band in the street began playing, and an equerry came up the stairs to tell them that the Prince of Wales would be with them in ten minutes.

'Say, if an American girl marries a prince, would she become a princess?' Dot asked Poppy, pulling a tendril of hair out of her cap and curling it round her finger.

'I should think so,' Poppy said. 'But don't hold out much hope of that – I rather think he might have to marry someone titled, like a duchess or a dame, or someone who's a princess already.'

'And someone British, I suppose,' Dot said.

'I expect so,' said Poppy. 'Did you know the royals are changing their name because it sounds too German?'

Dot nodded. 'So he'll want someone who'll back him up in Britishness, right?'

'Afraid so,' Poppy said. 'Hard luck, Dot.'

Tilly arrived carrying a big vase of wild flowers. 'I borrowed them from downstairs,' she said. 'I thought they'd make the ward look pretty.' Tilly went into the ward, positioned the flowers on the central table and came out again. 'Now,' she said to Poppy, 'tell us what we do if we're presented to this prince? Is there a law about what we're allowed to say?'

'I don't think there's a law . . .'

'He's a real prince of the royal blood!' Dot said, fanning herself with her hand. 'Just think of it. The legacy! The tradition!'

'As he passes us, do we curtsey, shake hands or prostrate ourselves on the floor?' Tilly asked.

'A curtsey will do,' said Poppy, giggling.

'And how do we do one of those?' Dot asked.

'One foot behind the other, bend from the knees and bow your head respectfully as you dip,' Poppy said, demonstrating it to them. 'Go as low as you can without falling over.'

'Is this right?' Dot and Tilly asked, bobbing up and down enthusiastically, one on each side of her.

'Very good!' Poppy said. Having so recently been in service, she didn't feel the need to practise.

There came some shouts from downstairs – cries of 'God save the King!' and 'God bless the Prince of Wales!' – and then the young man himself came up the central staircase. He was surrounded by important-looking people: hospital managers, field marshals, equerries and local dignitaries, also matrons and matrons-in-charge, and several elegantly dressed, aristocratic-looking ladies.

He was very handsome, Poppy thought, tall and sensitive-looking. Not a bit like his bluff, bearded father.

The crowd applauded, bowed and curtseyed as the Prince passed, but when he went right into Ward 5, most of his entourage stood respectfully to one side while he went to have a private word with several of the boys – including Tibs, Poppy was pleased to see. She hoped the royal visitor would be able to bring a smile to his face.

In fewer than ten minutes, the Prince was out again and the crowd, bowing and bobbing as before, clapped him all the way down the stairs and out towards his next appointment in Calais, for he was visiting as many hospitals as he could. Even royalty, Poppy reflected, were doing their bit for the war.

'Pearson!'

As the crowd dispersed, Poppy was just about to go over and ask Tibs what the Prince had said, when she heard Sister calling her.

'We have two more visitors waiting downstairs,' Sister said. Poppy looked at her, puzzled. Sister added, 'For Private Burroughs – Tibs, as you call him.'

'Yes?' Poppy said, very surprised. 'Are they his family?'

'Well, it's his mother and a younger woman who I took to be his sister. They arrived here just before the Prince, and I thought they'd be better waiting in one of the side rooms, out of the fray.'

'Do you want me to go and get them?'

'Would you? And perhaps you wouldn't mind preparing them for what's happened to his feet, just so they don't have too much of a shock. His mother's in a bit of a nervous state and his sister seems traumatised by everything she's seen here. When they've spoken to their boy, please ask them to kindly come and chat to me and I can tell them more fully about his injuries and his expected recovery.'

Poppy said she would, then went downstairs to where Mrs Burroughs and a young woman were waiting in a side room. Introducing herself as one of the VADs who were looking after Tibs, she asked if they'd had a good journey over and if they were staying at the hostel in town.

Mrs Burroughs answered Poppy's questions in a distracted manner, then said that they'd like to see Tibs straight away. 'You see, dear, we're terribly anxious,' she went on, 'because he's hardly told us anything about his injuries, just tried to make light of them. Why, Violet and me have been fretting half out of our skins about what might be wrong.'

'Violet!' Poppy said, turning to the girl in surprise. 'Then you're Tibs's fiancée.'

'I am,' she said. She blinked rapidly to disperse the tears which had suddenly appeared in her eyes. 'That is, I thought I was, until a week or so back when I had the strangest letter telling me about a French girl he'd met.' She shook her head and a few tears fell. 'I didn't even know he could speak French!'

'I'll give him French girl!' Mrs Burroughs said. 'He's got responsibilities, he has.' She looked meaningfully at

Violet, who smiled tremulously and put her hand on her stomach in a protective gesture.

'Oh! Are you . . . expecting?' Poppy asked.

Violet nodded. 'Tibs came home six months back,' she said in a low voice. 'He only had three days' leave and we were going to get married, but for one reason and another we didn't get round to it.'

'Young people . . .' Mrs Burroughs murmured.

'And then I found I was . . . I didn't tell Tibs because I thought he'd only fret about me. I told his ma, of course, but I made her swear she wouldn't say anything to him. I was going to surprise him when he next came home on leave.'

'But then he surprised us!' said Mrs Burroughs. 'Knocked us for six, he did. I was that ashamed! I could hardly believe my Tibs would do such a thing. French girl indeed!'

'Do you know who she is?' Violet interrupted. 'Is she someone who works here?'

'If she does, I'll be wanting a few words with her, I'll tell you that for nothing,' said Mrs Burroughs grimly.

Poppy took a deep breath. 'There is no girl.'

The other two stared at her.

'He made her up,' Poppy continued.

'But why would he do that?' Violet asked.

'Because he's been quite badly injured and he thought you, Violet, shouldn't have to care for him for the rest of his life. He was offering you a way out.'

'Is it . . . is it his face?' his mother asked, pressing her hand against her mouth. 'Is he very badly disfigured?'

Poppy shook her head. 'Not at all. He had a gash on his cheek, but that's healing nicely, and so is his arm. No, it's his feet – his toes. Have you heard of trench foot?'

Both women nodded.

'Well, Tibs had it extremely badly.' Poppy gave them a moment to take this in, then added, 'Some of his toes had to be removed.'

Mrs Burroughs gasped.

'My poor Tibs!' said Violet.

'Yes, but bad though that is, Tibs has actually been quite lucky. Some boys end up with gangrene and need to have half their legs taken away,' Poppy said gently. 'The medical staff are hoping that they can save the rest of his toes, however, and his feet.'

'And if the treatment goes all right, will he be able to walk?' Violet asked.

'He should be able to walk with sticks,' said Poppy, 'but his feet don't look very pretty. You must prepare yourselves.'

The two women exchanged glances, smiling bravely at each other.

'Oh, just his toes,' said his mother, her voice shaky with relief. 'You don't have to look at them if you don't want to. It's not like his ears or his jaw have been shot away to nothing.'

'That's more or less what one of the doctors said: that it's better to lose a toe than a nose.'

'I suppose so . . .' Violet said.

'Of course it is!' Mrs Burroughs agreed.

'He thought you'd be horrified, Violet,' Poppy went on. 'He said he wouldn't be able to take you dancing any more.'

'Oh! How could he think I'm that shallow?' the girl said, her eyes filling with tears again. 'My darling Tibs, with all that going on and no one to comfort him.'

'And what about his other injuries?' Mrs Burroughs asked.

'He had a very nasty gunshot wound to his upper arm, but we've been irrigating that with an antiseptic solution so it shouldn't go gangrenous, and that seems to be working.'

The little group was silent for a while, each dealing with their own thoughts, and then Violet asked what she ought to do about the letter.

Poppy thought about it for a moment. 'I think it's probably best to forget all about it – pretend you've never received it,' she said then. 'So many hundreds of letters must go astray and this could easily be one of them.'

'You know for sure that what Tibs said isn't true?' Mrs Burroughs asked.

'He told me as much when we were writing it – he needed to dictate the letter to me, you see,' Poppy said. 'And I know he's been utterly miserable since he sent it.'

'There!' said Mrs Burroughs with some satisfaction.

Violet got to her feet. 'I just want to see him now. Will you let him know we're here?'

'Give me five minutes and then come up to Ward 5,' Poppy said.

Going back into the ward, she spoke to Sister to get her permission, put screens around Tibs's bed and told him he had visitors.

'I've just had the Prince of Wales,' he said. 'Who's next, then?'

'Someone even better.'

'Is it the King?'

'No, it's your ma – and Violet,' Poppy said.

His face lit up, and then it fell. 'But they can't . . . I told Violet that . . .'

'Tibs, they've been terribly worried. They've come all the way from England to see you.'

'How did Violet know where I was?'

'Didn't you think that your fiancée might be in touch with your ma?'

'What will I say about the . . . ?'

'You don't have to say anything, because Violet never got your letter.' Poppy crossed her fingers behind her back. 'She never got it, so she doesn't know a thing about your imaginary French girl.'

'Oh!'

'And I've told them about your toes and they haven't run away screaming. Besides, Violet is . . .'

But no, Poppy thought. She must let Violet tell him that herself.

Peeping through the screen, she saw Mrs Burroughs and Violet with Sister, and then Sister was leading them across the ward. Poppy gave Tibs a thumbs-up and, as the two visitors appeared, silently slipped out from between the screens.

'Everything all right there?' Sister Gradley enquired.

Poppy nodded, smiled, but couldn't speak for the lump in her throat.

Chapter Twelve

'*Pour les blessés!*' A French woman with a crate on her bicycle stopped Poppy as she was going into the hospital. '*Excusez-moi.*' The woman pointed at the wooden crate, which was full of rosy-pink apples. '*Pour les . . .* wounded.'

'That's very kind,' Poppy said, helping the woman lift it down. 'The boys will enjoy these very much.'

The woman looked at her enquiringly.

'*Les blessés* will . . .' Poppy hesitated. *Amour* seemed too strong a word, but she didn't know any other. '*Les blessés amour des pommes,*' she said, knowing that if it wasn't quite right, the woman would understand what she meant. She squeezed the woman's hand. '*Merci beaucoup.*'

'*Merci,*' the woman repeated, smiling and nodding.

This was the third time Poppy had been given something for the boys in her ward. Quite often someone, usually a person who lived locally, would be standing on the steps of the hospital with a home-made cake, a slab of chocolate or some knitted garment, waiting to give them to a nurse or orderly. The ward the gifts ended up in depended on who came along first.

People gave according to their means – a couple of flagons of home-brewed cider often turned up and never went amiss. Poppy had heard of one lucky Boulogne hospital which received a hamper sent from Fortnum and Mason in London every week, a grateful family's thank you for saving their son's life and returning him to Blighty. Ward 5 had never managed to secure a hamper, but they'd recently been given six chickens by a Belgian farmer who'd been forced to leave his land and didn't want his little flock to be appropriated by German troops. The chickens had been put in the backyard of the Casino Hospital and were pecking around happily, laying well and providing fresh eggs for the patients. As yet, there were no calls for them to be killed and eaten, but if they stopped producing eggs it might become a different story.

Lugging the crate upstairs, Poppy said good morning to Sister and the others, and took the apples into the little kitchen to wash them.

The Casino Hospital was going through a slightly quieter period, with one of the other hospitals in the same group taking all new casualties and the Casino concentrating on those it had already admitted. There was a backlog of men in the wards now: some blind, some paralysed, some with bad facial injuries, and some with severe psychological problems – men who'd been sent almost mad by the war. These sorts of injuries were proving extremely difficult to deal with, and a number of patients was waiting to have decisions made about their future.

Taking care of the boys currently in the beds took precedence, of course, but Matron-in-Charge had also requested a spring clean and spruce-up of the entire Casino Hospital. It needed it, for this – and all the other base hospitals along the coast – had been opened in haste, thinking that the war would be over within a year.

When Poppy went along the beds later, giving out apples, the doctors and surgeons were on their usual daily round. Poppy waited by Tibs's bed, wanting to hear what they were going to say about him, for she knew that although his right foot was healing well, the left one from which the toe had fallen (thinking of it then, she still felt a little queasy) was causing them concern. Generally, Tibs had made good progress since the visit from his mother and Violet and, following another operation to tidy up what was left of his toes, it was hoped that the feeling in his feet would soon be restored. This would mean he could return to England in time to marry Violet before the baby was born.

'Any changes, Private Burroughs?' the doctor asked. 'No new pains in your feet?'

'Not that I've noticed' came the reply.

'And how's his shoulder wound, Sister?'

'Healing very well with the new method, as are the wounds of the other patients using it,' Sister answered, because most of the military hospitals were now using the Carrel–Dakin system of cleansing and irrigation.

'Let's look at this left foot again then, Private Burroughs,' said the leading doctor, and Tibs's foot was lifted into the air to be examined. The doctor drew a pin from the lapel of his white coat and pushed it a little way into the ball of his foot.

'Ow!' said Tibs.

'Really?' said the doctor, rather surprised. 'You felt that, did you?' He lifted the foot again and pressed the point of the pin into a different part. 'If you'll forgive my doing this a couple more times . . .'

'Ow! That blo–' Tibs looked at Sister and amended what he'd been about to say. 'That blimmin' well hurt!'

'Really? Excellent news!' one of the other doctors said. 'It's catching up with your right foot at last.'

'It might be excellent for you,' said Tibs indignantly.

'My good fellow, if the sensation hadn't come back soon, you might have ended up having the whole foot off,' said another doctor.

A broad smile slowly spread across Tibs's face. 'But now it's all right, is it?' he asked.

'Indeed it seems to be. Three cheers for your left foot and keep up the good work!' said the first doctor.

Those boys in the nearby beds who'd overheard cheered enthusiastically.

That afternoon, Sister informed everyone that an injured German prisoner was going to be admitted to Ward 5. This caused a bit of a stir and much muttering.

'We need to play this down as much as possible,' she later advised her team of nurses and VADs. 'You know what some of the boys are like . . .'

Poppy nodded. Since the start of the war, tales about bloodthirsty Germans had spread from regiment to regiment, troop to troop, and pal to pal. Poppy had heard enough gruesome tales of beheadings, the robbing of dead bodies, the stealing of children and other horrors to fill a book. She tried to keep an open mind, however, quite certain that German soldiers heard similar tall tales of atrocities inflicted by Allied troops.

Some of the boys of Ward 5, fresh from the fighting, didn't have quite such open minds, however. By teatime that afternoon, several had got together and produced a poster bearing the slogan THE ONLY GOOD GERMAN IS A DEAD ONE, which they proposed to put on the noticeboard.

Sister, quite furious, tore it in half. 'Really, I thought better of you,' she said, rounding on Privates Tasker and Bingley, the two ringleaders.

'Well, everyone knows that Germans are like wild men,' Private Bingley said. 'They're uncivilised. They eat dogs!'

'Oh, for heaven's sake!' Sister said. 'You shouldn't believe everything you hear!'

'But what's Fritz doing here anyway?' Private Tasker, who'd lost a leg and two brothers in the war, asked indignantly. 'He's taking up bed space that should belong to one of our boys.'

Sister tutted. 'He most certainly is not. I won't have such talk.'

'But where's he come from?' Tasker asked.

'I believe all the rest of his patrol was killed in a mining explosion,' Sister said. 'He was listed as missing. A couple of days after the explosion, he was found by one of our men in a dugout, more dead than alive, and taken prisoner. The German ward in the usual hospital for prisoners of war is full, so we've got him here.'

'Where's he going when he's better then?' Private Tasker asked grudgingly.

'The Ritz?' suggested Private Bingley.

Sister looked at them severely. 'If he gets back on his feet, and if he can stand the journey, he'll be sent to a prisoner-of-war camp in England.'

'A Blighty ticket before me!' Bingley said. 'Not fair.'

'Now,' Sister said, 'that's quite enough. This boy is some mother's son. Let's show him that we're civilised.'

Not all the boys of Ward 5 wanted to be civilised, however. They muttered and complained behind Sister's back, saying that the nurses weren't going to be safe with a German about and he'd have to be guarded day and night or chained to his bed.

'He's probably a spy,' Private Tasker said. 'He'll come in pretending his legs are broken and get out of bed at night to creep around and look in our lockers.'

'I want my bed moved as far away from him as possible,' Private Bingley said. 'I don't want to be garrotted while I sleep.'

Even Poppy began to wonder if the new prisoner of war might turn out to be trouble, like her friend Jameson's German officer in Netley, who'd given Jameson a gold ring and then asked her to pass on confidential information.

As soon as Dieter Brandt was wheeled in, however, pale and still after the amputation of an arm and looking about fourteen, everything changed. He'd been in the bottom of a trench for two days and then had to wait at the back of the queue to be operated on, because Allied officers and Tommies were always dealt with first.

The waiting around meant that Dieter had lost a considerable amount of blood. In addition to the missing arm, he had several big shards of shrapnel in his chest, one of which had penetrated a lung. This caused him to struggle and wheeze with every breath as he tried to draw air into his body.

He slept for almost two days, waking now and again to take water or milk in a feeder cup. Poppy usually gave him this, for Sister thought that because she was closest to him in age compared to the other VADs, he might be less nervous of her. When he did open his eyes properly, though, he obviously didn't know where he was and shied away from Poppy, regarding her with so much alarm that Sister said he'd probably been told the English would try to poison him if he was captured.

'It's all right,' Poppy said to him soothingly. '*Kamerad* . . . friend,' she said, for one of the orderlies had told her a few words of German.

Sister came over. 'Are you in pain, Dieter? Is there anything you want?'

He shuddered, looking terrified.

'You're quite all right here. Safe. It's good . . . *gut*,' Sister said. 'You'll come to no harm.'

After two days, propped by pillows and struggling to breathe, Dieter sat up and looked around him. His skin was as pale and thin as tissue paper and his eyes were a pale, watery blue. He shuddered and flinched at every noise in the ward – every dropped bowl or sudden shout – and those of the boys who'd glimpsed him through the screens reported to the others that he was scared of his own shadow and no more than a kid.

Private Bingley was heard to say scornfully, 'Look at the state of him. No wonder they're losing!'

Private Tasker, who had a son of Dieter's age, snapped back, 'You can shut up. They never should have taken him in the army in the first place.'

Two or three days passed and Dieter, though still hardly able to breathe, became a little bolder. He asked for one of the screens to be moved so that he could see out into the ward, and the other patients, curious to see a German up close, came and looked at him. One of them said, '*Guten Morgen*' and taught the others how to say it, too, so that every so often a head would pop around the screen and wish Dieter good morning, no matter if it was actually the evening, and this made him smile.

Several of the boys – the Welsh ones who were in choirs at home – sang 'Silent Night' to him, for although it wasn't anywhere near Christmas, the orderly said that it was a German carol and he'd like it. Tibs gave Dieter his apple, which he'd been saving, Private Tasker gave him a square of chocolate, while one of the others mimed writing a letter and offered him a British field postcard to send home. This caused an eager reaction from Dieter, and Poppy was sent to find the orderly who could speak German, so that between them they could write and tell his mother that he wasn't missing, but captured and at present receiving treatment in a hospital.

'When can Dieter have the operation to remove the shrapnel in his lung?' Poppy asked Sister, who began shaking her head before the question was half out.

'I'm afraid he won't be having one.'

'Why? Because he's German?'

'No, no!' Sister said. 'Because the shrapnel's in an impossible place, piercing his lung. The doctors saw from the last X-ray that there are ulcers forming around it already.'

'Then he won't live?'

'No, Pearson. I'm afraid not,' Sister said. 'Try not to get too attached to him.'

In fact, Poppy had seen that, day by day, he was growing weaker. His skin was taking on a blueish tinge and it was becoming more and more difficult for him to draw breath. When the boys acted the fool to make him laugh, it doubled him over with pain, and at last Sister had to put a stop to it.

Dieter became feverish, his temperature rising alarmingly, and Poppy was told to sponge him with tepid water in order to cool him down. He stopped eating and grew more frail, and even the offer of a soft-boiled egg for breakfast didn't tempt him. His pillows were removed, he signalled for the screens to be put back around him, and he lay inside them as flat and lifeless as he'd been when he was first brought in.

Every day when Poppy went into the ward, she thought he might be dead and would prepare herself accordingly. She didn't take her half-day off because she was quite sure that he'd die while she was absent, and she often spent off-duty hours reading or writing letters by his bedside. She asked the night VAD to come and wake her if Dieter suddenly got worse.

He struggled on, too weak to even turn his head, suffering so much that Poppy prayed he would die quickly. Now that the screens were back in place, those men who were 'up patients' tiptoed past his bed and took care to speak quietly when they were nearby. When the doctors did their rounds they always looked in on him, but came out shaking their heads.

If it had been a Tommy who'd been so ill, Poppy knew that Sister would have tried to arrange for his mother to come over and see him before the end, but of course nothing could be done for a German boy. She worried about the field postcard they'd sent to his mother. The poor woman would have heard from his commanding officer that he was missing believed dead, then received the card saying he was safe in hospital. Soon she'd have to hear all over again that he really *was* dead, and might even think the whole thing was a cruel joke on the part of wicked English nurses.

One day, when Poppy was in the kitchen boiling up water for the boys' afternoon cup of tea, Dieter quietly died. Poppy had very much wanted to be there when he passed, had hoped for some last words that might be written down and one day sent on to his people, but it seemed that he'd simply found the effort of breathing too great and decided not to do it any longer.

Dieter's coffin could hardly go out of the ward with a Union Jack covering it, and no one remembered seeing a German flag in the hospital, so in the end Sister draped the wooden casket in a plain white sheet. As it was carried out by two orderlies, the boys in the ward once again sang 'Silent Night'.

That afternoon there were no jokes or high jinks from the boys in Ward 5.

Chapter Thirteen

Casino Hospital,
Nr Boulogne-sur-Mer,
France

18th May 1916

Dear Miss Luttrell,
How kind of you to send the bedsocks so promptly, and I
must apologise for my slowness in writing to thank you.
Please tell your comforts group that the socks were very
well received by our boys – and the ward certainly looks
a gayer place with a stripy bedsock on the end of each
plastered leg.

We have been very busy here, with convoys arriving
from all over the place, bringing in all nationalities. We
had a German lad who sadly died, and the next ward
to ours has some Indian fellows. There are Chinese,

Russian and Congolese casualties as well – they've all been fighting or working alongside our own boys. The sister in the next ward tries to find each man's national flag to pin on the wall and make them feel at home, but says it is becoming more and more difficult.

Today I am going out with friends and we are having a whole day out! These are two American girls, Dot and Tilly, trained nurses at a hospital just down the road, who are very conscientious about their work but also great fun.

What do you think about this? American nurses are allowed to wear a little make-up. Also, they can go out to music halls and other entertainments with officers and (most annoyingly of all) are allowed to go dancing! Does that seem fair? All the British nurses and VADs are very cross about it and I think most sisters would agree with them, but, of course, these are army regulations and the sisters would never go against them. Someone spoke to our matron about dancing a couple of days ago and she said that the ban is for our own good, to ensure that nurses are respected and kept in high regard by the people of whichever country they're in. Really! It's not as if we're going to dance the cancan in the street.

My friends are waiting so I will close now, hoping this finds you as well as it leaves me.

With every good wish,

Poppy xxx

Poppy addressed the envelope. The only trouble with writing to Miss Luttrell, she'd found, was that she lived in Mayfield, where Poppy had worked for the de Vere family and fallen in love with Freddie. This meant that writing that one simple word on the envelope, *Mayfield*, brought everything back to her.

But she would not let these memories spoil the treat of a day's outing with Dot and Tilly, she resolved, putting on her outdoor uniform and leaving the hospital.

She'd been told that her two friends would be outside and presumed they'd be waiting on the steps. When she came out, however, she couldn't see them.

The area was bustling, as usual, with soldiers, nurses and all manner of vehicles. Some of these were motorised, some horse drawn, and there was also a handcart being pushed by a worried-looking man, with table, chairs, cushions, crates, bedsteads and mattresses – seemingly the entire contents of a small house – piled high upon it. Perched precariously on the very top were a dog in a basket and a child. Poppy, who'd seen such scenes in Boulogne before, knew it was either a refugee French or Belgian family who'd been moved on by the Germans. They'd be hoping to find a room in town perhaps, or – if they were lucky – obtain places on a boat bound for England.

Ten working horses went across the square, two by two, and a car hooted several times. Poppy stared at it, thinking how terribly stylish it was, with its hood back so that it was open to the elements. She'd never been in a private car – it wasn't the sort of thing that parlour-maids or VADs did.

The driver of the car hooted again, someone waved, and Poppy suddenly realised it was Dot sitting behind the wheel with Tilly alongside her. They'd hooted to try and attract Poppy's attention.

She ran over. 'What are you doing?'

'Getting ready for our day out,' Tilly said. 'Are you ready?'

'But *a car*!' Poppy stood back to admire it once more. 'Whose is it? Where did you get it?'

'It's a hospital car – someone donated it,' Dot said. 'It's been at the mechanic's having something new fitted, and they said I could test it out before it goes back to the pool.'

'But do you know how to drive?'

'Of course,' Dot said airily. 'Nothing to it. You just crank the handle to start the engine and jump in.'

'Or you get a good-looking guy to crank the car for you,' Tilly said. 'They love to do it because it makes them look muscular and strong.'

Poppy laughed. 'Shall I get in then?'

'You'd better, girl!' Dot said.

'Unless you'd rather run behind,' Tilly added.

Poppy climbed into the back of the car, holding on to the seat with one hand and a rope handle with the other. 'Is it really safe?'

'As safe as houses,' Dot called over her shoulder.

'Houses outside the war zone, that is,' Tilly shouted back.

'Where are we going?'

'Pop,' said Tilly.

'Poperinge,' Dot added. 'We've been before – we know the way.'

'Oh!' Poppy sank back on her seat, which was pale leather and as soft and comfortable as a feather bed. She'd heard of Poperinge because it was one of only two towns in Belgium which weren't under German occupation and, with its clubs and bars and restaurants, was a favourite place for soldiers to be billeted or take a few days' leave. It also had a vital railway line which brought men and equipment to the front line and took casualties out. 'Are we allowed to go so far?' she asked.

'Sure,' said Tilly, tying a chiffon scarf over her nurse's cap to stop it getting blown away.

'We're on a mission,' said Dot. 'We've been asked to give the car a run, and you're helping us.'

'How exciting!' Poppy said.

She looked out of the window, trying to relax. The sensation of being driven was new to her, however, and she began to feel a little as she had done on board the ship coming over. The road was bumpy, with many potholes and craters which caused Dot to swerve, and there was a considerable amount of traffic: private ambulances, trucks, army cars, even a tank. Was this the same tank she'd seen before, Poppy wondered, or were there more around now?

They wound their way through a wood then several villages and farmyards, once passing a regiment of men, their uniforms smart and buttons bright, marching in strict formation in the same direction. Seeing three smiling nurses in a car with the hood down, several of the Tommies risked getting a reprimand from their commanding officer to shout, 'Give us a lift, sweetheart?' or 'Got room for a small one?' as they passed.

'Poor lambs,' Dot said as the car sped on. 'All so eager to get into the fight. They have absolutely no idea of what's ahead of them.'

'I know,' said Poppy, leaning forward to speak. 'And now I think about it, it seems to me that I haven't seen a man without some sort of horrid injury for months.'

'Apart from the doctors,' Dot put in.

'Yes, apart from the doctors,' Poppy agreed, suddenly thinking of Michael Archer and smiling to herself.

'And the orderlies, of course,' said Tilly. 'But they're utterly ancient, so they hardly count.'

They went through more small villages. The Germans had come perilously close to two or three of these, causing the houses and smallholdings to be abandoned by the owners, and then looted. There were no sheep or cows to be seen, just one tethered donkey in a field, staring at the horizon. Who was coming to feed it? Poppy wondered.

In the background, far away, the distant booming of big guns could be heard, and rising puffs of smoke on the horizon showed where shells were bursting. The three girls fell silent, all probably thinking the same thing: it was a beautiful spring morning, the blossom was on the trees, and men were dying or being horribly maimed just a short distance away. It all seemed quite preposterous.

They came to a small farm with a handwritten sign which said, *ENGLIS TOMMIS COME HERE FOR COCOA.*

'Oh, do look,' Tilly said. 'How perfectly quaint. Do let's stop for cocoa and meet some English Tommies.'

'Impossible!' Dot said. 'There's no trusting a motor car. If we stop halfway to Pop, there's no guarantee that we'll be able to get it started again.'

'So how do we know this car will get us home all right?' Poppy asked anxiously, knowing that although the American nurses had certain privileges, *she* had to be back in the hospital no later than nine o'clock.

'My dear girl,' said Dot, 'if the car misbehaves in Pop, then we'll have the cream of the world's brave soldiers clamouring to help us. In fact,' she added, 'I'm praying it *will* misbehave in Pop.'

The countryside grew bleaker and Poppy saw evidence of recent battles: blackened sticks that had once been trees, scorched earth, dwellings reduced to a tumble of bricks.

Rounding a corner, the car approached a lay-by in the road, an area of scrubbed earth and meagre grass. Lying flat out, their heads on their kitbags, were about twenty British Tommies. Back from weary days at the front, dirty, bloodied and battle-weary, it looked as if they'd simply dropped down as soon as they'd reached safety. They were so still that anyone might have thought them dead – except for one man, who was sitting with his pad upon his knee, writing a letter, and who hailed the girls with a wave as they drove by.

'Oh gosh,' Tilly said. 'Those poor chaps look totally done in.'

'Why d'you think they have to sleep there, though?' Poppy asked.

Tilly shrugged. 'They probably got orders to retreat from the front line, but there was no transport available for them.'

'One of our patients said that his platoon spent two nights sleeping in a barn waiting for someone to come for them,' Dot said.

'I suppose they're so tired they don't care where they put their heads,' added Tilly.

Poppy wasn't at all sure how one was supposed to drive a car, but didn't think that Dot, swerving all over the place, making a grating noise as she drove up hills, speeding then braking sharply on corners, could be called a good driver. Feeling more and more nauseous, she closed her eyes and was very relieved when, at last, they arrived.

Poperinge was a small, neat town, with a pretty square and old buildings untouched by the surrounding battles. Dot drove into the marketplace, parked the car and they all climbed out.

Poppy, feeling a little unsteady on her feet, took several deep breaths.

Dot frowned. 'Say, you're looking awfully pale.'

'I feel a little pale . . .'

'A day out is going to do you good,' said Tilly.

'Perhaps,' Poppy murmured, 'but it's getting home that's bothering me.'

A small clutch of admirers quickly formed around both car and nurses, and the girls discussed what they should do whilst pretending to be unaware of them. Several boys offered to show them the town, buy them a beer or treat them to a 'slap-up meal', but after being studiously ignored, drifted away with last-try calls of 'Well, if you change your mind . . .'

'I think we should start by taking tea in Talbot House,' Tilly said.

'What's that?' Poppy asked.

'Well, it's kind of like a cross between a meeting place, a café and a club for Tommies and officers,' Tilly replied.

'It's all very friendly and open,' Dot put in. 'They tell you to leave your rank at the door. It has a lovely garden, and you can go there any time for refreshment.'

If there was one thing she could do with, Poppy thought, it was a cup of tea in a lovely garden, for she still wasn't feeling quite right.

They walked across the square and Tilly rang the door-bell of a substantial whitewashed house. The man who answered the door seemed rather surprised to see nurses standing there, but he ushered them through the hall towards the back kitchen, which overlooked the garden. 'Tea and biscuits for three, is it?'

'That would be lovely,' Dot said.

There was a large square table in the centre of the kitchen, around which sat five or six khaki-clad officers, who immediately leapt to their feet when the three girls came in.

In this way, Poppy came face to face with the man she'd thought could be the love of her life, Second Lieutenant Frederick de Vere, and immediately fainted.

Chapter Fourteen

When she came to, Poppy found she was sitting in the garden of Talbot House on a canvas chair with a rug over her knees. For a moment she stayed where she was, head bowed, eyes closed, wondering how she should act and what she would say next. How could she have done such a thing as pass out? What must everyone think? What must *he* think? Maybe she could just stay dumb and play dead . . .

'She hasn't been looking well since we arrived,' she heard Dot saying.

'I think she suffers from carsickness,' Tilly said. She lowered her voice. 'Might be the way you drive . . .'

And then – oh God! – it was Freddie speaking.

'It's Poppy, isn't it?' he said, and taking her hands, rubbed them to try to warm them. 'Poppy! Can you hear me?'

Not thinking about what might be the right thing to do, Poppy snatched her hands back from his. What gave him the right to think he could take her hand now, offer his help, after he'd sneaked off to marry someone else?

Cautiously, she lifted her head. 'I'm feeling much better now, thank you,' she said in a clipped voice, and put her hands under the blanket, so he couldn't reach them.

'Are you sure?' Freddie asked.

She didn't reply. How dare he sound so concerned?

'Hey, do you two know each other?' Dot asked.

'Yes, we do,' Freddie said.

'You've been in the Casino Hospital?' Tilly asked him.

'No. We know each other from . . . from England,' said Freddie.

Dot thrust out her hand. 'I'm Dorothy Manning from Chicago in the USA. And this is my friend Matilda Butt.'

'Dot and Tilly,' said Tilly.

'Freddie de Vere,' said Freddie, shaking her hand.

'Ah,' said Dot, while Tilly gave a little inward gasp, her eyes widening.

'Perhaps we could allow Poppy some air,' said Tilly, for two of the other officers had also come into the garden and were standing nearby, looking concerned.

'Yes. Yes, of course,' Freddie said. He looked at Poppy. 'If you're sure you're quite all right . . . ?'

'Perfectly all right, thank you,' Poppy said coldly, staring past him to the trees at the end of the garden.

'It was just travel-sickness,' Tilly said.

'Exactly,' said Dot. 'Trust us – we're nurses.'

The man who'd opened the door to them came out with a tray containing cups, saucers, a teapot and a plate of biscuits. 'We like to think that time spent in our garden will cure most ailments,' he said, 'so perhaps you ladies would like to stay out here in the fresh air with your tea.'

'That would be very nice,' Tilly said.

'Thank you for your concern. May we wish you all a very pleasant day,' Dot said. She was looking at Freddie as she spoke, the tone of her voice indicating that it was a closing remark.

The men went indoors, Freddie giving one or two backward glances as he retreated.

'That was *him*, wasn't it?' Dot said immediately after the door closed behind the men.

'Oh my!' said Tilly, fanning herself.

Poppy nodded and pressed her hands to her cheeks, which had now flushed pink. 'What a dolt I am!' she wailed. 'Fancy me fainting! He probably thinks it was the shock of seeing him.' She hesitated. 'And I suppose it was . . .'

'Nonsense,' Dot said. She set out the cups then poured the tea. 'We must put it all down to the car journey and travel-sickness. I'll drive home much more carefully.'

The three of them drank the tea during silent contemplation of the garden. This was lush and very pleasant, with spring flowers, ferns, grasses and fully grown trees gently shedding blossom. Poppy hardly saw these delights, however, because she was thinking of all the times she'd imagined meeting Freddie again and what she'd say to him when she did. Now it had actually happened, and she'd fainted like a wisp of a girl in a Victorian melodrama.

Tilly glanced back at the house. 'Ol' Freddie being here has altogether spoiled our visit,' she said. 'We would have shown you around the guest rooms, and there's a lovely little chapel up in the attic for boys to sit and think about things before they go back to the front, but I don't suppose you want to go in.'

Poppy shook her head. 'I'm sure it's all very nice, but I'd just like to get out of here.'

'Why, sure you do,' Tilly said.

'But I must say something to him when we go,' said Poppy to the other two. 'Something that will let him know how deeply upset and . . . and heartbroken I am.'

'What?' Tilly cried. 'Never!'

'We couldn't possibly allow you to do such a thing,' said Dot, sounding quite shocked. 'What we're going to do is finish our tea, take courteous leave of our host and his companions, then sail through the kitchen with our noses in the air. And your nose, Poppy, must be highest of all.'

'The other men will think we're real unfriendly, but it can't be helped,' said Tilly.

When the time could not be put off any longer, Poppy put down her teacup with slightly shaky hands, stood up and folded the rug.

'Ready?' Dot asked her.

'Ready,' she replied, though she didn't feel ready at all.

'Noses up!' Dot commanded and, with her leading the way, the three girls went into the kitchen, exchanged a pleasant remark or two with the chap who'd made the tea, and went to the front door.

Poppy, last in line, had reached the street and was turning to close the door when Freddie caught up with her.

'Poppy,' he said. 'Please! I simply can't let you go without apologising for my . . . for what happened.'

Poppy, looking at him, felt a great welling-up of indignation and couldn't speak.

'I was a complete cad, I know that,' he said. 'You've every right to hate me. You see,' he went on, ignoring Dot and Tilly, who had walked on a little way, 'I went home on leave and found that my mother had arranged it all – everything, down to the wedding rings and cake. There was just no escape.'

'But you didn't have to go through with it,' Poppy said.

'I know. I was a coward, but Miss Cardew and everyone else seemed to think it was what I'd wanted all along, so I made up my mind that I'd go through with it and it would be my sacrifice for the war.'

'How very noble of you,' she said stiffly.

'Please believe me. I did care for you, Poppy. I used to treasure those –'

Summoning all the self-control she could muster, Poppy raised her hand to indicate she didn't want to hear any more. 'Goodbye, Second Lieutenant de Vere.

May I offer my congratulations on your marriage,' she said, and then turned on her heel and went to join the other two.

'Jolly well done!' Tilly whispered as they walked down the street.

'Poise maintained, dignity preserved,' Dot said.

'Has he gone back inside?' Poppy asked, and getting the nod that he had, was at last free to burst into tears.

A couple of hours later, Poppy was feeling a little better. The three girls had found a restaurant selling Belgian specialities and had consumed hearty portions of chicken stew whilst dissecting the whole business of Freddie de Vere. Poppy didn't think it was likely that Dot and Tilly could appreciate the class distinctions between her and Freddie, because it wasn't the same in America, but they certainly all came to the same conclusion: Freddie de Vere was a mother's boy, a cad and a bounder. What was more, they all felt extremely sorry for Miss Cardew, who knew nothing of what had gone on.

'You're better off out of it,' Tilly said.

'Handsome men never make good husbands,' said Dot darkly.

After eating, they did a tour of the shops and Poppy bought some pieces of Belgian lace for her mother and aunt, and a chocolate chicken each for her sisters. She couldn't afford to buy one for herself, but was cheered by the thought that it could be months before she got a week's leave and she would almost certainly have eaten both of her sisters' chickens by then.

And so the day improved, with all three girls pretending not to enjoy the whistles and waves they received from the Tommies wherever they went. The officers were a little more subtle about showing their appreciation, but most were just out of the trenches and hadn't set eyes on a girl for several weeks, so were very keen to make an impression. Poppy couldn't really relax because she was too concerned about bumping into Freddie, so Dot or Tilly would go into shops and cafés beforehand and give them a once-over to make sure he wasn't there.

They went into the yard of Poperinge Town Hall and Dot told her about the condemned cell, which was just out of view. 'Prisoners have their last meal brought to them, then they confess their sins before being tied to that post over there . . .' she pointed, 'and shot.'

'That's a terrible business,' Tilly said.

'Do you mean German prisoners are shot here?' Poppy asked.

Dot shook her head. 'No. It's Allied soldiers who've deserted and been recaptured, or refused to carry out an order, or simply can't face another day of fighting.'

Poppy shook her head, hardly able to believe it. It was hard to imagine this happening so close to hand, in the centre of such a normal, popular little town.

'As if enough boys aren't being killed by the enemy,' Tilly said incredulously. 'Can you believe we shoot our own soldiers?'

Poppy thought of her brother Billy, who'd risked the firing squad to shoot himself rather than go over the top. 'It doesn't seem right. Just because someone's scared half out of their wits . . .'

'Do you think there's anyone in the condemned cell now?' Tilly asked.

'Bound to be,' Dot said. 'It's a horrible little hole – I've seen it. Stinking, freezing cold and running with rats.' Then she added, 'And afterwards, the commanding officers add to the all-round wrongness of it by writing to the boy's family and telling them that their son died a dishonourable death.'

'I call that putting the boot in,' Tilly said.

The girls stood in silence, contemplating the execution post, then Poppy said, 'Don't you think we ought to start for home soon, in case it takes us a while to get the car going?'

Dot nodded. 'So let's look around for a handsome and muscular man now . . .'

Chapter Fifteen

Poppy closed her eyes in the back of the car going back to Boulogne, tried to breathe evenly and told herself sternly that she did not feel sick.

Going over the meeting with Freddie in her mind, she covered first the fainting (oh, how foolish!), then the snatching away of her hands (terribly childish), and finally the aloof farewell at the door, which was the only part of seeing him that, though she did not feel good about it, she was reasonably content to recall. Yes, she'd concentrate on that and forget about the other parts. And at least their first meeting after his wedding had happened now, so any subsequent occasions would be easier. Perhaps.

Dot and Tilly were in the front seat of the car and singing at the tops of their voices as they drove along, so for perhaps half a minute none of the girls noticed that the engine had cut out. The car went slower and slower, however, and finally, spluttering, came to a halt.

'It's quite all right,' Dot said airily. 'It just wants water in the radiator. I should have put it in before we left Pop.' She got out, went into the boot and got a full can of water, then tried to undo the radiator cap. It was very hot to the touch, though, and she burned her hand and swore at it.

While this was going on, Poppy climbed out of the car and walked around it a few times to stretch her legs. No travel-sickness this time . . . maybe because she'd had her eyes shut. They must be about halfway home, she thought, and had ended up on a quiet stretch of road which was heavily wooded on both sides. Towards the east, sporadic bursts of shellfire could be seen and heard, each side trying to get in a final flurry of killing before sunset. The sky wasn't yet dark, but it was gloomy under the trees. How far did German snipers venture? she wondered. Who might be in those woods waiting for unwary travellers?

The radiator cap cooled enough to be removed and Dot poured the water into the radiator then screwed the cap back on.

This little job done, Tilly rummaged around on the floor of the car then held up the starting handle. 'Who's going to do this? Where's a Tommy when you want one?'

'Give it here,' Dot said, and she cranked the handle six or seven times without success.

Tilly tried, then Poppy, then Dot again.

Finally, Dot gave a squeal. 'It's the gas!' she cried. 'They told me I'd have enough to get to Pop and back, but we've run out!'

'Petrol? Isn't there a spare can of that in the boot, too?' Poppy asked.

They searched, but there wasn't.

Getting back in the car and sitting there in the gathering gloom, Poppy began to fear that they were all going to meet horrific ends: that a Zeppelin would come along and spot them, or a stray incendiary would burn up the woods all around them and they'd be trapped within walls of fire. The very best scenario she could think of was that they'd have to wait half the night to be rescued, then she'd get back to hospital to find herself charged for being Absent Without Leave – an offence that could lead to instant dismissal and an immediate return to the UK.

'I guess we'll just have to wait for an army lorry to come by and give us a tow,' Tilly said. 'But I'm surprised at you, Dorothy Manning, I really am. Fancy coming out here in the middle of a war and not making sure there was a spare can of gas in the back.'

'There are two of us in this front seat,' Dot retorted. 'You've got to take some of the responsibility.'

'If only you'd let me! You always insist on being in charge and going first . . .' Poppy leaned back on the seat and closed her eyes again.

Ten minutes or so went by. Poppy was wondering why the road was so much quieter than when they'd come along that morning – could it really be the same one? – and Tilly and Dot had argued themselves into an injured silence when, suddenly, behind them there came the sound of a thudding engine.

'Quick!' Dot said, the row forgotten.

'Stop that car!' said Tilly, scrambling out.

All three girls stood behind the car, arms poised ready to wave – and round the corner came a motorcycle and sidecar. Their arms drooped, disappointed, but the motorcycle pulled up and came to rest just beside them, its driver kitted out in a black leather motoring coat and boots, flying helmet and goggles.

'Can I help you at all?' asked a breathy and well-modulated female voice.

The girls were stunned into silence for a moment, then Dot said, 'Thank you, but not unless you're carrying a can of gas? Petrol, that is.'

'I'm afraid I'm not,' said the young woman, pushing the goggles back over her head.

'Oh!' said Tilly. 'I've seen photographs of you in the newspapers! You're part of Mairi and Elsie, aren't you?'

'Yes, I am,' she said, smiling. 'I'm the Mairi part.'

The four girls shook hands. Poppy had heard of Mairi and Elsie and their famous first-aid post – had even read a book about them, and admired them very much. Mairi had come over from England at the start of the war when she was eighteen. Between them, she and Elsie Knocker, a trained nurse, had set up their own little day hospital, as close as they could get to the front line. The men of the Belgian Army Third Division were stationed nearby and would come to them to be treated for minor conditions – boils and lesions, scrapes, toothache and twisted ankles – anything which might not be a battle wound but which was causing them pain or discomfort. The girls, with the help of some drivers, also ran two ambulance cars, picking up soldiers from all units who were badly injured and taking them to clearing stations.

'And where are you all from?' Mairi asked. 'You two are Americans, of course!' she added immediately. 'How marvellous that you're here working alongside us.'

The four of them briefly exchanged news and views, and Mairi asked where they were heading.

'Back to Boulogne,' said Dot.

Mairi pulled a rueful face. 'Not only have you run out of gas, but you're on the wrong road, I'm afraid. This is the road to Pervyse, where Elsie and I have our little outpost.'

Dot and Tilly glared at each other, and Poppy almost said she'd thought it wasn't the right road.

'Are we very far out of our way?' she asked instead, still worrying about being AWOL and getting bumped back to England.

'Not too far. I can lead you back to the crossroads and put you right. That is, I could if your car had any fuel.' She hesitated. 'I have some full cans back at the post. I could spare you a gallon, if you like.'

'That would be terrific, thank you,' Tilly said. 'We'd replace it, of course.'

'So, who's going to come with me in the sidecar to get it?'

'Me!' the three girls said together, and Poppy thought it was because Mairi didn't want to have to choose between the two American girls that she was picked.

As Poppy wriggled into the sidecar, Mairi consulted the small gold watch on her wrist. 'We'll be about half an hour,' she said, pulling her goggles down. 'Don't go away!'

Poppy found riding in the sidecar of a motorcycle more frightening, yet also more exhilarating, than being in a car. It was rather like a carousel ride, but a lot more fun. While she bounced up and down, hair flying everywhere and not in the least bit travel-sick, she thought about how much she would enjoy telling the boys in the ward about meeting Mairi Chisholm. There were always articles in the newspapers about the two famous young women, the only females allowed anywhere near the fighting.

They arrived at what had once been a small town, but which had been bombed into piles of rubble, with half-fallen houses and flattened walls. Trees were reduced to nothing more than sticks and there was barely a blade of grass to be seen. Mairi carefully drove into a building which was just two standing walls and a few steps leading down to a cellar.

'This is us,' she said. 'This is where we live.'

'Oh.' Poppy, shocked at the dilapidation and shabbiness of the place, didn't know what to say. She had heard of the girls' little hospital and pictured it as being clean and shiny, like a real one but in miniature. This was just a wreck.

'Sad, isn't it?' Mairi said. 'A few shells, a grenade or two and the whole place is flattened. It does well enough for us, though.'

Hearing Mairi's motorcycle arrive, a small collection of cats and kittens ran over the rubble to greet her.

'All yours?' Poppy asked, counting twelve.

Mairi nodded. 'They got left behind when their owners fled and we adopted them. Or they adopted us.' She bent down to ruffle tabby fur. 'I don't suppose anyone's fed them all day, because Elsie's gone to London to try and raise more money for bandages and medicines. We're frightfully hard up here, you see.' She smiled at Poppy, who, despite being surprised at the paucity of the place, was still a little star-struck at meeting her. 'I know you're anxious to get back with the petrol, but would you like to see inside our little sanctuary?'

'Oh, yes please!' Poppy said.

As she spoke, there was an almighty bang as a shell exploded and, quite close to, a cloud of smoke rose into the air and slowly dissipated, leaving the distinct smell of cordite.

'Aren't you very near the front line?' Poppy asked rather anxiously.

'Quite near. Occasionally we get a rogue shell close to us, but not often.'

There were two men in Belgian Army uniform waiting on a bench by the front door. Mairi looked at a bad cut on the forehead of one of them and said, translating to Poppy afterwards, that she wouldn't keep them too long. 'They'll wait all night if they have to,' she said to her. 'We're open all hours.'

They walked down a dozen steps into the cellar. Here there was more order. Crates provided storage for plasters, bandages, iodine and basic medical essentials. There were further crates and pallets doing a turn as tables, stools, and (with cushions on top) chairs. In the room beyond, two single hospital-style beds could be seen, and there was also a padlocked steel cabinet containing, Poppy supposed, drugs and medication.

'It's all very basic, I'm afraid, but it's bombproof,' Mairi said. 'Periodically we try and tidy up, but there's no space to put anything, and the men come in and out all day treading mud, and the cats cause havoc.' She picked up a small black and white cat. 'This one, Maisie, is in charge. She teaches the others to sit on the beam above the door and jump on the head of whoever comes in.'

Poppy laughed.

'Luckily the King was very good about it.'

'The King?' Poppy asked, astonished.

'King Albert of the Belgians – he came to visit and thank us for the work we're doing.'

'Oh!'

'Such a terribly nice man, and he didn't seem to mind a bit about Maisie.'

'Gosh! And what d'you do with yourselves when there are no patients to look after?'

'We make soup for the boys, and take it down the lines,' Mairi said. 'Or if there are no vegetables to make soup with, we make vats of cocoa. Sometimes we go out and collect bodies. Or name tags from bodies, I should say,' she added, seeing Poppy's face. 'Sometimes families have only heard that their boys are missing, so they keep hoping that they're still alive. If we find a dead Tommy with a name tag then we let his people know what's happened to him. It's terribly sad, but finding out the truth can come as a relief.'

'But don't you get shot at by the Germans?'

Mairi smiled. 'We have an arrangement. When Elsie and I go out to the trenches we wear red headscarves, and that shows the German commander that it's us and means they mustn't fire.'

'And can you trust them?' Poppy asked incredulously.

'Yes, we really can. It even gets quite jolly when we give out presents to our boys at Christmas or Easter. First we send over a nice message, tucked into the collar of our little dog, to say we're coming, and we go out carrying a placard saying, *All Germans are daft* or something silly. And the Germans put out a notice saying, *The English are bloody fools* or some such thing. Then someone will write, *Let's all go home!* or *Make mine a pint!* This makes everyone laugh and we're all good chums. For a little while, at least,' she added rather sadly.

'And do you treat everything here?'

'More or less.' Mairi nodded. 'Elsie's a fully trained nurse, so we can deal with everything from boils to broken limbs. Mostly, though, we treat the everyday things that don't quite merit a chap going into hospital.' She bent down to pick up a kitten who was climbing up her leather-clad leg and smiled at Poppy. 'But we'd better be getting on our way . . .'

> *Casino Hospital,*
> *Nr Boulogne-sur-Mer,*
> *France*

> *23rd May 1916*

Dearest Ma,
I think you must have read in the newspapers about those brave girls Elsie and Mairi and their little hospital. Well, I met Mairi today and I think it was even more of a thrill to see her than the Prince of Wales!

My next job is to find a moment to write to Billy. When I last heard from him he said he was waiting for a letter from you; have you written recently? I think he was concerned not to have had any word.

We are as busy as ever here with casualties from the front. Every man, every illness and every injury is different from the one that went before. You can have twenty men, each with a smashed-up leg, and they are all different types of injuries in different places, and so will differ in severity and subsequent treatment. In some cases the leg will have to come off up to the thigh, in others up to the knee will be enough, and in lucky ones the leg can be saved. It's just a case of the doctors making the right decision in the time available.

We had a man in last week who'd thrown back a grenade a little too late and lost most of his left arm because of it. He was tidied up at a clearing station (his arm was amputated) then he came to us and slept for a couple of days. When he woke, he realised that his wedding ring had gone along with his left arm, and asked if we could enquire for it at the clearing station! I had to explain that the ring had probably got lost when the grenade exploded, but that anyway the surgeons and theatre nurses were much too busy to search through amputated limbs in search of a ring. 'My missus will be that cross!' he said, and was worried about the loss of it, poor chap, but I assured him that she'd be so happy to see him that she wouldn't even notice.

Do write soon, Ma, and let me know how you all are. Much love,

Poppy

Chapter Sixteen

The young soldier had been brought into Ward 5 of the Casino Hospital because he had no label tied to him with any other destination, and the ambulance men didn't know what else to do with him. Somehow, during the process of being brought from battlefield to hospital, he'd also lost his jacket and trousers and now, wearing no more than a vest, long pants and a gold cross and chain, he was covered all over in dirt and grit. It coated his eyelids, stuck to his hair, filled his nostrils and ears, and had even got inside his mouth.

He didn't seem to have any life-threatening injuries, however, so Sister told Poppy to get the worst of the debris off him, and then let him sleep. He did sleep, but panted rather than breathed and woke every hour or so to scream that he was being buried alive. When he did this, he would kick off the coverlet and tear at the sheets and make great clawing movements with his hands.

Sister asked him what had happened, but he just looked at her, agitated and wild-eyed, and shook his head.

'I don't believe it'll help him to talk about it yet,' Sister said to Poppy as they stood beside his bed. 'He's still in shock. He should go in a quiet room where he can't disturb the others, really. But then again, being here in the midst of things may help him to realise he's with us now and quite safe.' She sighed. 'The medical textbooks I read when I was training didn't cover this type of thing.'

Their patient gave a sudden, very loud shriek, startling the rest of the ward. 'Help me!' he cried. 'I can't see! Can't hear!'

'You're all right now,' Sister began.

'I can't breathe!' he screamed, then, seemingly exhausted, slumped and closed his eyes.

Every so often the whole performance was repeated – so much so that some of the other Ward 5 patients who also suffered with their nerves began to get agitated and jumpy, and Sister decided that he should be moved to the small single room usually kept for men with bad facial injuries. This, however, seemed to make him worse, and Poppy, who had a half-day off and was going out with Tilly and Dot, was worried in case Sister asked her to forgo this and stay to keep an eye on him. Happily, one of the orderlies volunteered instead.

At noon Poppy gave out the dinner trays as usual, then said goodbye to the boys in the ward ('Who're you going off to meet, then?' and 'Have you got a date, nurse?' came the cries). She went to her basement cubicle to put on her outdoor uniform. She had a choice between straw hat and felt hat, and deliberated for some minutes as to which she should wear, but eventually decided that although the straw was more flattering, it wasn't yet summery enough for it to be worn.

'Tilly and I have got the car again,' Dot announced, coming into Poppy's cubicle and perching on her bed, 'and today we're going on a picnic!'

'How lovely,' Poppy said. 'But I don't know what I can contribute.'

'Oh, we've been collecting bits and pieces,' said Tilly, for the two American girls got frequent food parcels from home. 'I'm sure none of us will go hungry.'

Poppy thought about it for a while, then, deciding that the chocolate chickens she'd bought for Jane and Mary would have to be sacrificed to the day's enjoyment, put them into her canvas bag.

The car was parked in the square outside the hospital, a different car from last time and not quite so large.

'We've already had a gallon of gas delivered to Mairi,' Dot said, 'and we've got a spare can in the boot. Just in case.'

As Poppy was about to get in the back of the car, there was a shout of 'Hello, Pearson!'.

All three girls turned to see Doctor Michael Archer coming across the square, waving and smiling.

'Well, who's this?' Tilly murmured, but Poppy didn't have time to answer before he reached them.

'You three young ladies aren't neglecting your duties, I hope!'

'Certainly not,' Poppy said. 'We've done our duties today. We've got an afternoon off.'

Dot, standing next to her, gave a little false cough.

'Oh, sorry,' Poppy said. 'These are my friends, Nurse Dorothy Manning and Nurse Matilda Butt. This is Doctor Michael Archer.'

'Do call me Michael, please.'

'Certainly,' Dot said immediately. 'And you must call us by our first names, Dot and Tilly.'

Michael raised his eyebrows at Poppy. 'What, even call Pearson here by her first name?'

'Of course!' Dot said. 'We never call her anything but Poppy.'

'Ah!' Michael said. 'When we were at Netley, the first names of VADs and nurses were kept a deadly secret. So it's Poppy, is it?'

Poppy, embarrassed, didn't reply.

Looking from one to the other, Tilly laughed. 'You Brits are so terribly formal. You need to loosen up a little!'

Michael seemed amused. 'Then I'm sure you're the very pair to teach us. And where are you off to on this lovely day?'

'A picnic,' Dot said. 'Would you like to come?'

Poppy gave a little gasp of surprise, partly at Dot's forwardness and partly because everyone knew that doctors and nurses weren't supposed to fraternise.

'Well,' came his answer, 'it just so happens that a doctor friend and I had planned to go on a little excursion this afternoon.'

'But we're not allowed to –' Poppy began.

'But *we* are!' Tilly said.

'And if it also just so happened that three hard-working nurses were, on their time off, picnicking in the same place at the same time as two equally hard-working doctors, who could be blamed? No one!' said Michael. 'Now, where are you going, exactly?'

Dot, who had a rough map with her, showed him and pointed out the bluebell woods. 'We might be slightly late in the year for them,' she said, 'but apparently it's always very pleasant in that area, and there's a lake and so on.'

'I hope to see you there, then,' Michael said. He looked at Poppy, gave her something which was suspiciously like a wink and went on his way.

'What a lovely boy!' Dot said, looking after him admiringly. 'How come you never told us about him?'

'Because there's nothing to tell,' Poppy said. She thought about it. 'Not really.'

'Hmm ... *Not really*, the girl says,' Tilly remarked. 'There's a wealth of meaning in those two words.'

'I don't know what you mean!'

'Well,' said Tilly, 'if you're really sure there's nothing to tell, kindly point him in my direction.'

*

It turned out that the bluebells were almost over, but under the pine trees they still showed as a rolling carpet of hazy blue. Dot, searching for the perfect picnic spot, led them on and on around the lake and Poppy, breathing in the subtle fragrance of woodland flowers, felt almost relaxed for the first time in ages. She'd been so busy, so caught up in the patients' lives, that there had hardly been time to consider her own.

So, she thought, she'd loved Freddie and it hadn't worked out, but listening to other girls' talk, how many first loves ever did? There would be other romances, surely? She'd work as hard as she could, see out the war (however long that took), become a proper, trained nurse – and, after that, there would be plenty of time to think about romance and love and all those sorts of things. A wisp of a thought about Michael Archer crept into her mind and was quickly dismissed. No, she didn't want to fall in love now – it was too dangerous. She could remember her friend Jameson saying back in Netley that a girl only had to get a diamond ring on her finger for her fiancé to be announced as Missing. Besides, Michael was such a joker – how could a girl ever believe anything he said?

'Hello!' Michael Archer's voice echoed across the lake, and the nurses turned to wave to the two figures who'd appeared a couple of hundred yards behind them. 'Are you nurses ready to be accidentally bumped into by two doctors?'

'Well, sure!' Dot called back.

Michael Archer and his colleague, James Turner, had both qualified as doctors at the same time. Whereas Michael was of average height, James was very tall with a shock of fair hair and a broad Scottish accent which Dot seemed to find very appealing. In a kitbag James carried a small primus stove in a fireproof box, a tin kettle and a brown glazed teapot, and the tea he brewed was served in condensed-milk tin mugs. Once the tea was made and drunk, Michael, using the same kettle, soft-boiled five eggs he'd found under a farmyard hedge, and buttered slices of fresh white bread, which he cut into soldiers.

Dot and Tilly were enchanted – and Poppy was quite enchanted, too, for of all the boys she knew (admittedly not many) she didn't know any who could so much as butter a slice of bread for themselves, let alone boil an egg.

When the eggs and soldiers had been eaten, Tilly and Dot brought out their contribution to the picnic – ham and pickles, a Swiss roll and a jar of honey – and Poppy put her two chocolate chickens into the mix.

The conversation naturally turned to things medical, and Poppy struggled to keep up, for she was the only one who had no proper qualifications. She was deeply interested, however, in hearing the others discuss the latest findings on such things as gas blindness, trauma and gangrene, and to learn that medics had even begun doing blood transfusions person-to-person on the field.

They spoke about some of the boys they'd looked after who'd pulled through despite having terrible injuries, and Poppy mentioned the boy who'd come in only that morning, who was rather disrupting the whole ward.

'He arrived in the back of an ambulance with no visible wounds,' she said. 'We don't even know where he's from.'

'What did he look like?' James asked.

'It's hard to say,' Poppy replied. 'He'd lost his jacket and trousers along the way and he was a kind of dusty mud colour all over. His skin was the same colour as his hair. He even had mud in his mouth, poor chap. Oh, and he was wearing a gold cross and chain.'

'I saw him. He came through our clearing station!' Michael exclaimed. He thought for a moment, then he said, 'I remember now – he was in a mining accident. I examined him, prescribed a sedative and tied a label to his toe giving my recommendation. Private O'Toole, his name was. I remembered that because my CO has the same name.'

'The label must have come off somewhere down the line,' Poppy said. 'But do you know what actually happened to him? I'm sure Sister would be really interested.'

'I was told that O'Toole was working with a dozen other lads tunnelling under the German lines in order to blow them to Kingdom Come. Something went drastically wrong, there was a huge explosion and the whole lot – boys, spades, shells and kit – went right up in the air and crashed down again. Most of the lads working there were killed instantly. Two crawled out, but they died of their injuries shortly after. An absolutely tragic story.' Michael shook his head sadly. 'But then this whole foul thing is one big tragedy.'

'How horrendous. So it was all for nothing?' Dot asked.

Michael nodded. 'The tunnel they were digging turned out to be a mass grave.'

'So how on earth did this O'Toole chap get out?' Poppy asked.

'Apparently he was six feet under and two sandbags had fallen across him, pinning him down. His arm was sticking up, though, and they just saw the tips of his fingers showing above the ground. He had the sense to wriggle them so they knew he was still alive.'

Tilly gasped. 'How did he breathe?'

'Another sandbag had fallen just in front of him, leaving a pocket of air around his face. He was buried for four or five hours before anyone could reach him, so I'm not surprised he's got the jitters now.'

'I'd better tell Sister that the little back room without windows isn't the right place for him then . . .'

'No! He'd be much better off on the balcony, out in the fresh air,' Michael said.

There was a pause in the general conversation, and James began showing Dot and Tilly how the primus stove worked.

'So, Pearson. Your name's Poppy, then, is it?' Michael said.

'Have you really only just found out?'

He smiled his wide smile. 'Of course not,' he said. 'I asked your brother as soon as I met him.' He paused. 'I think I shall still call you Pearson, however. It reminds me of Netley and how we met.'

Poppy smiled, for some reason absurdly pleased with this answer.

'How is your brother, by the way? Is he behaving himself?'

'He seems all right,' Poppy said. 'He's put his name down to be a stretcher-bearer. As long as he doesn't have to fight again, I think he'll be all right. He's just not cut out to be a soldier, to kill people.'

'When it comes to it, not many lads are. But unfortunately most of them don't find that out until they reach the front.'

The two doctors had only four hours off duty so went back to their hospital shortly after the picnic. Michael bid a friendly goodbye to all three girls, and said he hoped he'd see them soon, but it was Poppy he was looking at and Poppy's hand he pressed as he said his farewells. Dot and Tilly didn't see, either, the kiss which he blew her from the other side of the lake, which she was too flustered to return.

When Poppy got back to the hospital, there was a letter from Billy waiting for her.

Hi Sis

How are you doing? All quiet here, which means that at the moment i don't have to go out picking up bodies. We have some blokes from the Australian army billeted next to us: big lads, they are twice the size of us so it's good that they are on are side. They call us Poms or Pommies (dunno why) and are allways making jokes and larking about. When it comes to a ten mile trek tho, or digging out an eight foot deep trench, they are the boys.

I have heard from ma now. It was a funny letter with prayers in it she wants me to say evry night. She said two women she knows have lost there sons and she goes to church twice a day lighting candles and so on so that i don't die. What good this will do i don't no.

Do you ever get any ciggies donated for your patients? I was wondering if you could send me one or two packets, if you have any spare. They are good currency here you can swop a couple for a bar of chocolate or whatever. I could also do with a few thick pares of socks not for me but to sell on, the Australians don't seem to have stuff like that and there is money to be made if you keep your wits about you. Make sure they are big sizes.

The guns are booming again, they never bloody stop do they. Let me know what you are up to (don't forget the ciggies).

Love, Billy.

Sister had his bed moved to the far end of the ward and, if he couldn't sleep at night, he'd stand by the open window, throw his arms back and breathe deeply. Sister realised it was something to do with the trauma he'd been through, but he wouldn't talk about it and said he'd always liked being out in the fresh air.

He'd palled up with Private Booker, who was the only other patient in Ward 5 who didn't have a visible injury. Booker had been bayoneted in the stomach and the exterior wound had healed well. His injury apparently superficial, he was being kept under observation until the doctors were sure he didn't have any internal injuries. He was quite happy to be observed in this way and was hoping that it might continue for the rest of the war. To this end, he'd taken to getting into bed and uttering faint moans whenever there was a doctor around.

Sister already had her suspicions about him and was all for packing him back to his unit for light duties, but the doctors weren't certain yet. His case was helped, too, by the fact that the hospital wasn't terribly busy at that time and he could be spared a bed. A rumour had begun, however, about masses of weapons being stockpiled for a Big Push, and everyone knew when that started it would be a case of freeing up as many beds as quickly as possible for the casualties that would come in day and night. In the meantime, Privates Booker and O'Toole, both seemingly quiet and inoffensive chaps, would sit on the balcony and do jigsaws together, or – as they were both 'up patients' – put on their 'hospital blues' and go out for a walk.

After dinner on this particular day, Poppy was sent out on an errand by Sister. She came back along the promenade, squinting in the sunshine across the Channel to see if she could glimpse the white cliffs of the English coastline.

There was a small café bar along the prom which, although run by a French couple, always contained lots of British customers: boys who'd just arrived in France, those going on leave, mothers and fathers over here to visit their recovering sons and staying at one of the hostels, and anyone else trying to kill a little time. Poppy glanced in, but the windows were steamed up and at first she thought she must be mistaken in what she saw. The two figures at the bar looked like Privates O'Toole and Booker, but they both had bandages round their heads and O'Toole had what looked like a broken arm in a splint. There was also a pair of wooden crutches propped against the bar.

Poppy stared through the plate glass, confused. Had they both had an accident she hadn't heard about? But she'd seen them only that morning and they'd seemed perfectly all right then.

Suddenly, Private O'Toole saw Poppy, and, nudging his chum, quickly whipped off the bandages round his head, which had been preformed into a ready-made turban. His head was revealed, completely wound-free.

Mystified, Poppy went in.

'Don't tell Sister!' said Private Booker as she approached.

'It won't happen again,' said Private O'Toole. 'It was just a joke.'

'What was?' Poppy asked. She frowned. 'Why are you covered in bandages?'

'Sit down, nurse!' Private O'Toole said, removing the splint from his arm. 'Have a nice French coffee, won't you?'

'Just tell me what you're doing here,' Poppy said, quite sternly, for although she had absolutely no status at all within the hierarchy of the hospital, the boys in beds seemed to make little distinction between VADs, staff nurses and sisters; all were called 'nurse' and usually deferred to as figures of authority. 'And why do you look as if you've just come from a clearing station?'

There was a long pause.

'The thing is,' Private Booker began, 'all the other chaps in the ward have injuries that show . . .'

'So when they go out and about, they get looked after,' finished Private O'Toole.

'What d'you mean?'

'Well, they're heroes, ain't they? They get treated to a cup of tea here, have a pat on the head there, and half a crown or a shilling gets slipped into their back pocket.'

Private Booker nodded towards the bar. 'They sometimes get a nice little shot of whisky or a glass of Calvados.'

'But we get nothing!' Private O'Toole said. 'People can't see what we've got wrong with us, so they treat us like malingerers.'

'Malingerers, is it?' Poppy raised her eyebrows meaningfully.

'People ask us what injuries we've had and want to know when we're going back to the front. I tell 'em I had a bayonet in me guts and I'm still under the doctor, but I don't think they believe me.'

'I tell them I was buried alive,' Private O'Toole said, 'but unless they can actually see you've got something wrong – like a bandaged limb with a bit o' blood on it – they're not really interested.'

Both of them smiled uneasily at Poppy.

'No harm done. We just thought we'd get ourselves a bit o' pocket money, see,' Private Booker said.

'You won't tell Sister, will you?' Private O'Toole put in quickly. 'We won't do it again, will we, Booker?'

'Certainly we won't,' Private Booker said. 'Wouldn't dream of it.'

'Sister would have a fit,' Poppy said. 'The boys from her ward, out begging!' She tried not to smile as she reached across the table. 'Come on, let's have the bandages and the splint, then . . . and the crutches.'

'Here, just to show willing,' Private Booker said, and he got out a handful of money and put it on the table. 'This is what we've got so far today.'

Poppy scooped up the mixture of francs and sixpences. 'I'll put it in the Ward 5 treats box.'

When Poppy got back to the ward, she found the men – and one man especially – in a good mood, for the doctors had decided that, as Tibs had now felt some sensation in both feet, he was recovered enough to go home, as long as he took things easy and promised to massage his feet every day.

'Tibs has got his Blighty ticket!' Private Bingley shouted down the ward. 'Some devils have all the luck!'

Sister, who was taking temperatures at the time, gave him a look. 'Lucky?' Poppy heard her saying, 'If you think losing most of your toes is lucky . . .'

If there was an element of luck involved, Poppy thought, Tibs was lucky not to have lost either of his big toes, for she'd been told that if either of these went then one's body was thrown off balance, making walking much more difficult. As it was, however, slowly and leaning on a walking stick, Tibs intended to lead Violet down the aisle. Much teasing of the bridegroom went on, and the boys made a card for Tibs full of doubtful jokes about him already having had his wedding night some seven months previously.

Three other convalescent boys from Ward 5 went on the Red Cross ship with Tibs, and almost immediately four new casualties arrived. Two of these were Belgian soldiers who were taken under the wing of one of the older VADs, who spoke fluent Flemish. One newcomer was a sergeant major who took his job seriously and whose bark could be heard from one end of the ward to the other, and the last was a lanky lad of about seventeen, who had a gunshot wound to his arm.

As usual, the long-term men in the ward left the new boys alone for a couple of days. This allowed them to sleep as much as they wanted, then slowly come to terms with where they were and what injuries they had. Once they were sitting up and looking around them, the long-term residents of the ward would come and call on them, asking to know all the latest from the front and how the new boys thought the war was going.

They didn't get much information out of Private Casey, the young lad, apart from the fact that he'd signed on under age and wished to God that he hadn't. There was a great difference between him and the other young chaps in the ward, who were always ragging each other or making up marching songs with double – smutty – meanings. While they larked about, Private Casey would stare at them, baffled by their banter and trying desperately to keep up with what they were talking about.

Seeing this happening, Sister asked Poppy to keep an eye on Private Casey and, if she had a moment, go and chat to him, so some afternoons Poppy would sit by his bed. There she'd darn bedsocks or sew buttons on pyjamas while Private Casey told her about his life at home before he'd joined up. He'd lived on a farm with his mother and father in Somerset, where they'd kept a herd of cows and delivered milk to their neighbours in the surrounding countryside, and he wanted nothing more than to be back there.

'All I had to worry about there was whether our cows were giving enough milk and when to run them with the bull,' he told Poppy one afternoon.

'If it was just you and your dad on the farm, couldn't you have got a certificate to say you were in a reserved occupation?' she asked him.

He shook his head. 'I didn't even try. I got given a white feather, see, and it made me feel that bad that I weren't fighting.'

'But you were under age!'

'I told the woman that, but she wouldn't have it.'

Poppy briefly thought of Miss Luttrell, who'd once handed out feathers to all and sundry without much thought for the consequences of her actions.

'She said I was a strong lad and I had no excuse not to be fighting for my country.'

Poppy sighed. 'And so I suppose you went to the recruiting office . . .'

'That's right, and when the quartermaster asked me how old I was, I forgot to lie and said seventeen. He said to go away and come back the next day when I was eighteen. And that's what I did.' He shuddered. 'And then I started to get trained how to kill people and I didn't like it one bit.' He was quiet for a moment. 'But it was seeing those poor horses struck down in battle that was the worst thing of all. You see, they'd already come and taken away two of ours from the farm – they wanted them for war work. So Dad and I were managing with just one horse each to pull the carts.'

'That must have been hard work for the two horses left behind,' Poppy said.

He nodded and his bottom lip trembled. 'But we kept telling each other that our horses would be doing sterling work at the front, pulling ambulances and bringing men in to safety. But when I got here and saw all the poor things piled up dead on the ground . . .' His eyes filled with tears and Poppy passed him a handkerchief. After a moment, he continued, 'We were taken to our billet, which was on land which had just been fought over, and the first thing I saw was a horse like our Gertie – with the same markings.' He paused to blow his nose. 'But a shell had exploded nearby and that poor horse had been blown right up into a tree and was just hanging there over a branch, dead.'

Poppy bit back tears of sympathy. 'That's terrible.'

'There were dead horses everywhere I looked, and others just about alive but suffering terrible injuries, and not nearly enough veterinary men to treat them, and I thought, what are we all doing here? Oh, I do want to go home!' As he said this, he turned his head into his pillow and began weeping.

Poppy patted his shoulder, then pulled the screens around his bed and went to get him a hot drink. She'd speak to Sister, she decided – see if they could perhaps try and get Private Casey's mother and father over to give him a boost, give him something to look forward to. He couldn't possibly go back to the front line as he was.

In the kitchen, Poppy put the kettle on the gas and heard someone come in behind her.

'Poppy?' a hesitant voice said.

Wheeling around, she came face-to-face with Essie Matthews, her best friend from Netley.

'Matthews!' she said in amazement. 'Have you been posted here? How lovely!'

But Matthews, although she hugged her back, did not look as if it was a lovely occasion at all.

Chapter Eighteen

'What a surprise! Have you just arrived? Which ward are you on?'

A handful of questions tripped off Poppy's tongue, but none of them received an answer. Matthews just stood there, rather flustered, looking as if she wanted to speak, starting sentences but not continuing them.

There was a pause, then Poppy, realising Matthews couldn't find the right words and that there was something wrong, said more urgently, 'What is it? I know something's wrong.' When it still seemed as if Matthews might prevaricate, she added, 'Please! Just say it.'

Matthews tried to compose her face. 'Poppy, I'm very much afraid it's your brother. It's Billy.'

Poppy could not speak for a moment, just stared at her friend. Then she said, 'Not . . . ?' She shook her head. 'Not dead?'

Matthews nodded. 'Yes. I'm afraid he *is* dead. There's no mistake. Oh, Poppy, I'm so terribly sorry.' She put her arms about Poppy, who swayed against her.

'Are you sure? Could there be any doubt about it? I mean, has anyone seen him or has he just been posted as Missing? Might he have been captured?'

'No. His . . . his body came in. I saw it briefly.'

Please, please, don't let it be another self-inflicted wound, Poppy thought. 'Do you know what actually happened to him? Don't tell me he did it himself?'

Matthews shook her head. 'I don't know very much at all, except he had multiple injuries.'

'Where are you stationed? Where was he?'

'I'm in No. 1 General Hospital in Étretat.' Poppy looked blank, so she added, 'It's on the coast, north of here, about three hours away by train. There are lots of Australian units billeted there.'

'Oh, yes,' Poppy said, remembering Billy's letter.

'I'm in a surgical ward,' Matthews said, 'and I was on night duty when he was brought in.'

'And was it self- . . . Did he do it himself?' Poppy asked. Oh, the shame of it if he had.

'That's just it,' Matthews said. 'I don't know exactly what his injuries were. Someone was checking the tags of those who were unconscious and I heard someone call out, "William Pearson, dead on arrival". I tried to get over to find out more, but we were really busy. There'd been some sort of skirmish going on, there were a dozen badly injured boys on stretchers and people were running about all over the place. You know what it's like.'

Poppy nodded.

'There was someone else who was DOA and he and your brother were taken away so the doctors could get on with saving the living.'

There was a metal stool in the kitchen and Poppy, feeling sick and weak, sat down on it.

'So, before I went off duty this morning I found out where his unit was and went to see his commanding officer,' Matthews continued. 'I told him that you and I were great friends, and that your ma is a widow and it was going to be a terrible shock for you both, and he spoke to some bigwig who gave me permission to come up here and tell you, rather than sending a telegram.' Poppy didn't say anything and Matthews added, 'Awfully good of them really, considering I'd only been there a while. And if you want to be at the funeral and see where he's buried, you can come back to Étretat with me. I've got a permission slip for you to give your matron and a travel warrant.'

'But didn't Billy's CO say how he died?' Poppy asked. 'Didn't he give you any sort of hint?'

Matthews shook her head. 'You know how inscrutable those army types are. Everything's kept secret.'

'Because I . . . I don't want to go to his funeral if it's just to have a lecture about what a wicked thing he may have done – cowardice under fire and letting his country down and all that.'

Matthews shook her head. 'I wish I could have found out more.' She closed her eyes, as if to concentrate the better. 'I think he came in on his own . . . I don't remember anyone else from his unit coming in injured.'

'And he really is dead? There's no possibility of a mistake?'

'I'm afraid he really is,' Matthews said. 'Look, there's no need to come back with me if you don't feel up to it.'

Poppy sighed, wondering what to do for the best. 'I think I must,' she said after a little while. 'I could get a photograph of his grave – Ma would want that.' She gave a cry. 'Oh, what about Ma? However will I tell her?'

'We can catch a train back to Étretat this afternoon.'

Poppy looked at her friend closely, as if suddenly noticing it was her and not just a messenger. 'God, Matthews, you look done in.'

'That's what night duty does for you,' Matthews said. 'But I can sleep on the train going back.'

Poppy smiled at her. 'It's lovely to see you,' she said, and then burst into tears. 'But I do wish you hadn't had to come.'

It took under an hour for Poppy to explain the situation to Sister, pack a few things in a bag, put on her outdoor uniform and get down to the main station in Boulogne with Matthews. She felt dead and hollow inside, not knowing quite how a girl who was going to her brother's funeral should act. Once she knew what he'd done, it would be easier. She'd know whether to be ashamed of him, to hang her head at the graveside and not meet anyone's eye, or to be upright and proud of the brave stretcher-bearer who'd perhaps died whilst bringing in a wounded man. But when she found out the truth, how was she going to word the letter to her mother? Would she have to lie to her, the way she'd done before?

The train was over an hour late getting away, but this wasn't unusual considering the numbers of horses, trucks, crates of machinery, provisions and equipment also going to Étretat, as well as Australian or British soldiers either being newly posted to the area or returning to their units after a few days' leave.

Neither of the girls slept at first, because they had much to talk about: the progress of the war, the ways in which their hospitals over here differed from Netley, the merits of night duty, the scandalous lives of the silent movie stars and how annoying it was that they weren't allowed to go out socially with either Tommies or officers. And, of course, there was the topic of romance . . .

'Have you met someone, then?' Poppy wanted to know.

'I have!' Matthews said. 'And it's all happened so fast that I haven't even had time to write and tell you.'

'Since you've been over here?'

Matthews nodded. 'Right in Étretat!' she said. 'Stanley was in my ward and was just about to go convalescent when I arrived.'

'And what happened? How did you get together?'

'Well, Stanley's a great joker,' Matthews said, smiling. 'I served him soup and he declared he'd fallen madly in love with me at first sight. Then he took my hand and said he wasn't going to let it go until I promised to marry him.'

'Never!'

'And of course I knew I'd get into fearful trouble with Sister if she found us holding hands over the soup, so I said I'd marry him just to get away. But . . .'

'But?' prompted Poppy.

'But I did awfully like the look of him and he made me laugh, so when he said a few days later that he'd really meant what he said, I went along with things so as not to spoil the fun.' She smiled. 'Well, one thing led to another and we arranged to meet in secret, and now he wants to get married on our next home leave.'

'Matthews! How exciting.'

'Yes, it is, but I'm terribly worried about Sister finding out we're seeing each other, because if she does it'll mean instant dismissal and I'll be sent home.'

'And even if you get married . . .'

'Exactly,' Matthews carried on. 'They don't allow married girls to nurse if their husbands are serving soldiers.' She shook her head. 'And terrible though it is in some ways, I love being over here and doing my bit.' She heaved a sigh. 'But what about you?'

Poppy shook her head. 'Nothing so romantic, I'm afraid. But I did bump into Freddie over here . . .'

And she told Matthews all about the trip to Poperinge, the embarrassing fainting and the way Freddie had come after her, and went on and on about the whys and the wherefores at (she realised later) rather boring length until Matthews's eyelids closed and, leaning her head against the windowpane, she fell asleep.

Once there was no one to have a conversation with, Poppy did not have to keep up the pretence of being brave any longer. She closed her eyes and, her thoughts returning to Billy, tears began to seep from under her eyelids, causing the others in their carriage to studiously look the other way. Had she let Billy down and hastened his death by encouraging him to join up? Why, she'd even thought about giving him a white feather! She was his older sister – shouldn't she have looked after him better?

She thought back to when Billy had been born. She could remember, just, the day her mother had given her a penny to go to Mrs Dickenson's corner shop for two ounces of pear drops. Years later, Ma had told her that this had been a trick to get her out of the house for the last few, noisy moments of the birth. Mrs Dickenson had been waiting for her, and given the little girl a job of counting packets of sugar. When Poppy eventually went home, she was told that a stork had visited the house and delivered a baby. 'We knew straight away it was a boy,' her ma had said, 'because he was wrapped in a blue blanket.'

She thought about them growing up: all the times that she'd stood up for Billy, fought his fights, prevented Ma from finding out about some naughtiness, argued his case with his teachers . . . all for nothing! Hardening her heart, she vowed that if he had disgraced the family with a death that was self-inflicted, then she wouldn't bear it on her own; she'd tell everyone exactly what had happened.

A moment later, though, she changed her mind. Why should her mother suffer because of what Billy had done? It would be hard enough for Ma finding out that Billy had died, let alone that he'd disgraced his family and his country. No, unless her mother found out some other way, she would cover for him, as she'd done before – as she'd done all their lives.

It was almost dark when they stopped at a tiny station whose name had been obliterated. Here two Irish soldiers began to run along the platform shouting, 'Kitchener's dead! Kitchener's dead!'

Those who'd been sleeping, including Matthews, roused themselves, made for the windows, leaned out and asked for more news. Everyone knew, of course, of Field Marshal Kitchener, the army officer with the bristling moustache, whose commanding slogan *YOUR KING AND COUNTRY NEED YOU* was on recruitment posters throughout the land. At length one of the soldiers stopped outside their carriage and told them the rest of the story. Earl Kitchener, it seemed, had been on a trip to Russia on a British warship when it had been sunk by a German mine. Nearly all on board, 650 or so men, had drowned. Although the Earl was not a popular man, this was a truly shocking event. No one on that train slept for the rest of the journey, for they were too busy discussing what had happened, and whether the Germans had known Kitchener was on the warship or had just been extremely fortunate.

The train halted several times along the way to load and unload, so a journey which should have taken only three hours took much longer. No one seemed in the least bit surprised at this, however – there was a war on, after all.

When they eventually reached No. 1 General Hospital, it was eleven o'clock at night. This was much too late for an audience with Billy's commanding officer, so Matthews found a spare mattress, some bedding and just enough space on the floor of her tent to fit Poppy in.

Beyond weary now, Poppy got into bed without even washing her face and tried to sleep. She'd given up praying for things, because her prayers never seemed to be granted. Besides, she always thought, if a prayer was anything to do with winning the war, the Germans were praying to the same God as they were, so how was that going to work? The Germans weren't going to be bothered about her brother, though, so she prayed most fervently that, the following day, she might discover that Billy had died a proper and patriotic death.

Chapter Nineteen

Matthews had taken two nights' leave and didn't have to be on duty the following day, so took Poppy into her hospital canteen for breakfast. Poppy, however, couldn't eat – even a small square of buttered toast got stuck in her throat and refused to go down. Sitting with Matthews in the mess tent, she felt rather scared of what Billy's CO might say to her and desperately hoped that he wouldn't preach or give her a lecture on her brother's shortcomings. Ought she to stand up for Billy, she wondered, try to make excuses for him, even though whatever was said against him was probably true?

'They'll be burying your brother and five others at two o'clock,' Matthews said. 'You should be able to get a train straight back to Boulogne after that.'

Poppy nodded absently. She'd been longing and longing to see Matthews and to talk to her about all the things going on in her life, but now she was actually sitting alongside her she couldn't think of anything except Billy.

She went in a hospital car to Billy's unit, which was resting up some distance from where the main action was. This gave her some hope. Before, when he'd shot himself in the foot, it was because he'd panicked when he'd been ordered to go over the top. This time, there would have been no such order to terrify him. That, surely, must be good news?

'Major Hawkins will see you now,' said the young clerk, gesturing for her to go into the makeshift office which had been constructed under an archway of a bridge.

Poppy went in, heart in mouth.

'You are Private Pearson's sister?'

'Yes, I am, sir.'

The CO looked younger than she'd thought such a senior officer would be, but grander somehow, and with a well-spoken, de Vere sort of accent. They shook hands.

'I'm so very sorry about your brother, Miss Pearson,' he said, gesturing for Poppy to sit opposite him. 'I haven't written to your mother yet. I wondered if you might prefer to do it.'

'I think so, sir. Thank you.' Poppy looked at him, expectant and nervous.

'Now, about Private Pearson.' The major looked at her appraisingly. 'We officers used to use the expression "a bit of a lad" when we were talking about your brother.'

'Yes, sir.' Poppy's mouth was dry.

'And his death rather bears that out.'

Poppy swallowed hard. 'I don't actually know yet how he died, sir.'

'Ah.' He paused. 'Well, it's quite simple. He went out at night trying to catch rabbits and he fell over a cliff.'

Poppy, stunned, tried to take this in.

'He died on impact, I'm afraid.'

Poppy couldn't speak for two full minutes. 'R . . . rabbits?' she said then.

'Indeed. Apparently there's a bit of a black market in the old bunnies – to supplement the soldiers' rations, don't you know? The Australians are especially keen on them – cook 'em up in their billycans.'

'So . . .' Poppy hesitated and then spoke in a rush. 'So if my brother had lived, would he have been up on a charge for this . . . this rabbit business?'

Major Hawkins shook his head. 'As far as I know, there's no army rule about not hunting rabbits. It's just a rather needless way to die.'

Poppy began to cry a little, partly from sadness at Billy's unnecessary demise, and partly from relief that he hadn't died a coward's death.

'Private Billy Pearson wasn't exactly an ideal soldier,' Major Hawkins went on, 'but he was resourceful, enterprising and cheerful, which was all to his good.'

'Yes, sir. Thank you.'

'Your mother is a widow, I understand?'

'Yes, she is.'

The CO started writing on the form he had before him. 'Because of that, I'm entering in the records that your brother died as the result of an accident whilst on patrol.' He glanced across at Poppy. 'This means that your mother will get a small army pension. It's not a great consolation for the loss of a son, but it's something.'

'Thank you, sir,' Poppy said again.

'And you'll write to your mother to tell her the news?' he enquired.

Poppy nodded.

'You can tell her the absolute truth: that Billy would have died instantly of his injuries and not suffered in any way. There are worse deaths.' He gave a wry smile. 'But as a VAD you would know that, of course.'

'I'll tell her, sir. And I've arranged to have a photograph taken of Billy's grave, which I'll send her,' she added, for Matthews had said that Stanley had a camera and would do this. She got to her feet and shook hands with the major, relieved that the interview was at an end. 'Thank you very much indeed, sir.'

'Not at all. And, once again, please extend my condolences to your family.'

By three o'clock that afternoon, Poppy was on the train going back to Boulogne. Billy's funeral ceremony had been solemn but brief; with so many young men dying, it was not good for morale to make much of a fuss about their ends. The six elm coffins were put one by one into the earth, a wooden cross was erected with each boy's name, and a hymn was sung by those few people present. All the men buried, five Tommies and one officer, had the same simple wooden cross.

'It all could have been much worse,' Poppy had said as she and Matthews hugged goodbye at the station.

'Lucky that his CO turned out to be such a decent sort.'

Poppy nodded. 'That's the official story, then: Billy died whilst on patrol. Ma will be happy with that.' She checked herself. 'Well, not happy . . .'

'I know what you mean,' Matthews said.

Poppy's ma was much on her mind, so when the train halted and did not seem about to start again, Poppy got out her notebook to try and formulate a letter. It was an awful task to undertake – a terrible, impossible task – but Poppy thought that the sooner Ma knew the worst, the sooner she could start to recover.

Nr Boulogne-sur-Mer,
France

6th June 1916

Dearest Ma,
I'm afraid I have some terrible news – just about the worst news that a girl could ever have to tell her ma. It's

about our Billy. I am so sorry to say that he died as a result of an accident on 5ᵗʰ June. I spoke to his commanding officer today and have just attended his funeral. I'm getting a photograph of his grave so you can see what a pretty spot it's in, in a quiet space under some trees. My friend Matthews, who's working nearby, has promised to put some flowers on the grave for us and will see that it stays tidy.

Billy's commanding officer was very nice about him, saying that he always found him resourceful and cheerful. Apparently Billy was on night patrol when he tumbled over a cliff. He would hardly have known anything about it – he died instantly and would not have suffered any pain. When I think about some of the terrible injuries on the poor boys I've nursed through their final hours, I was most relieved to hear this.

Ma, we have both worried about Billy in the past, but please be consoled to know that he died in the service of his country. When this terrible war is over, I will bring you over here with the girls, and we can plant a rose bush on Billy's grave and say a proper goodbye to him. I am trying to remember our Billy as he was when I saw him going to catch his troopship in Southampton – marching down the road, pleased to be among his mates and proud to be doing his bit, a carnation sticking out of the barrel of his rifle and winking at every girl he passed.

I will write again soon, but in the meantime please write back to me so that I know you've received this letter. Jane and Mary will be very upset about their big brother, but tell them from me that they must be brave and grown-up, and look after you.

Dearest Ma, I am thinking of you and sending all my love and strength.

Poppy x

The train did not start again on its journey for an hour, so Poppy had time to read through the letter and make small changes here and there. It did not, she thought, say anything that could possibly help, but she knew now that ultimately there were no words that could console a woman who'd lost her son.

Arriving at the docks at Boulogne, Poppy found them busier than ever, making her wonder once more about the Big Push that everyone was talking about. No one knew the start date or which section of the front line would see this action, but there was no doubting the fact that something immense was about to happen. Hundreds of men were arriving on troopships, new platoons were being formed, vehicles were undergoing checks, and recovering casualties were rejoining their regiments earlier than they would have been normally, in order to leave more space in the hospitals.

There was a small fruit and vegetable market in the square and Poppy stopped to buy cherries from one of the black-shawled women seated on the steps of the church. Beside her was a cage containing half a dozen live wild rabbits, and Poppy, who loved rabbits and could never have eaten one, was thinking to herself that she'd quite like to buy them and free them to make up for those that Billy had caught, when she heard a familiar voice.

'Pearson!'

She turned, recognising the voice at once. 'Doctor Archer!'

'Michael,' he said.

'Yes. Michael,' Poppy repeated, thinking, what the heck – if Dot and Tilly could, then she could, too.

'Out enjoying yourself in the sunshine?'

'Not really.'

'I suppose you're buying food for another picnic!' he said jovially.

Poppy shook her head. 'No. I've just attended my brother's funeral.'

As soon as she said this she regretted being so direct, for his smile dropped and his silver-grey eyes clouded over.

'No! Gosh, I'm so terribly sorry. I shouldn't have . . . That's what happens when you try to be witty. I'd never have said something like that if I'd known.'

Poppy immediately felt remorseful. She touched his arm. 'No, *I'm* sorry. I shouldn't have been so blunt.'

'Then we're both sorry,' he said, and he put his hand lightly over hers.

They stared at each other for a second or two, then Poppy removed her hand and stepped back. Feeling self-conscious, she rustled the bag she held and offered him a cherry.

He shook his head. 'Please, tell me about your brother.' He lowered his voice. 'It wasn't self-inflicted?'

'No, thank goodness,' Poppy said. 'Not this time. What happened was a rather Billy thing, though: he was chasing rabbits when he fell off a cliff. He was stationed at Étretat,' she added, for there were no cliffs around Boulogne.

'And how did his CO take this?' As Michael spoke, he absent-mindedly took a cherry from the bag Poppy was holding.

'He was very good about it. He filled in some paper-work to say that Billy had died whilst on night patrol.' She smiled a wan smile. 'He didn't mention rabbits in the report at all.'

'That was jolly decent of him.' He took another cherry. 'But I'm really most terribly sorry, Pearson.'

'Yes. Thank you.' Poppy felt the beginnings of tears again and strove to change the subject. 'But what are you doing in Boulogne?'

'I'm getting our dogs ready.'

'What dogs?'

'We have six attached to our medical unit,' he said, popping another cherry into his mouth.

'To run errands?'

'Almost. After a battle they're sent out to no-man's-land with little packs on their backs, looking for survivors.'

'Really?'

He nodded. 'They carry bandages, iodine and a nip of whisky, so that a man can help himself if a dog turns up before a stretcher-bearer arrives. I've come to see if any new packs came over on today's boats.'

'Are these dogs needed for the Push?' Poppy asked.

He nodded. 'Ah yes, the Push. Wherever. Whenever.'

'So you don't know when it will be, either?'

'Does anyone?' He shook his head and took another cherry.

'I'd better get back to the hospital – that is, if I'm to have any cherries left.'

'Oh. Sorry, have I been eating them?'

Poppy nodded. 'You said you didn't want one, then began scoffing the lot.'

They both laughed.

'But shall I see you soon?' he asked.

'I expect so,' Poppy said and, despite the mission she'd been on, felt a little stirring of pleasure.

Chapter Twenty

Sister Gradley and the staff of Ward 5 were very sympathetic about Billy's death. At this point, almost two years into the war, nearly everyone had a friend or family member who'd been killed, and those left behind were forced to find methods of coping with death and its aftermath.

By the middle of June, conscription in the UK had been extended to include married men between 18 and 41, leave for medical staff had been stopped, and a good number of convalescent men had been returned to their units in readiness for the Big Push. Private Casey was still in Ward 5, however, and – mostly because he hadn't had Poppy to speak to for a few days – seemed to have slipped further into his shell. His introversion was made worse by the other boys in the ward having found out what he did in civvy life, then making up a song about a milkman, which they'd taken to singing to him whenever he ventured from his bed:

'I am a jolly milkman,
I'm laughing all day long,
If you come down to my farm
Then you'd hear my song.'

The joke was supposed to be that Private Casey was not in any way jolly, but out of place and rather sad. After a day or two of the song, with an extra verse that Sister Gradley said was quite disgraceful and never wanted to hear again, the ringleaders were spoken to and asked to stop.

'Don't you think he should be given a Blighty ticket?' Poppy said to Nurse Hunt one morning when they were on a bandaging round. 'He's just not made for fighting.'

'That's as maybe, but I'm afraid that excuse won't wash with the War Office,' Nurse Hunt said, shaking her head. ' "Not made for fighting" might apply to a lot of boys in the trenches.'

'I know,' Poppy said. 'And Private Casey wasn't even called up. He enlisted early and lied about his age. It was only when he got here that he realised he should never have done it.'

Nurse sighed wearily. 'The times I hear that.'

She and Poppy moved on to the next bed, which contained the most serious case on the ward at this time: young Sergeant Miller, who'd suffered a severe wound to the stomach wall, which had left some of his vital organs exposed. He wasn't expected to survive, but was in hospital to be kept comfortable and be helped towards as peaceful an end as possible. Ideally he would have gone home to England, but it wasn't thought that he'd survive the sea journey. So, with his father serving in Gallipoli, his mother had been told of his plight and asked to come to Boulogne quickly to say her last good-byes. Under Sister's instructions, Poppy had written to her a week or so back, telling her as gently as possible that her son was not expected to live and giving her the address of the nearest relatives' hostel.

Poppy, who liked Sergeant Miller very much and had helped with his bandaging before, was nonetheless relieved when Nurse Hunt decided that it might be better for Sister Gradley to help her with the dressings rather than Poppy. This was because his wound was particularly ghastly and Sister, who was much quicker and defter than anyone else, was able to trim a full eight minutes off the painful re-dressing time that he had to endure.

Later that morning, Poppy went downstairs to see if the post from Blighty had arrived. She was feeling rather anxious, as it was over a week ago that she'd written to her mother telling her about Billy, and so far she'd had no reply.

She collected Ward 5's letters and parcels and took them back upstairs (to the usual mighty cheer from the ward), where she found three letters with her name on. Each of these had the sender's address on the back, however, and none was from her mother. One was from Matthews, another from Tibs and a third from Sergeant Miller's mother.

Poppy distributed the post and the parcels to the boys, tried to cheer up those who hadn't received anything, and opened the letter from Tibs and his new wife. This contained a note thanking everyone for their good wishes, and a photograph presumably taken outside their local town hall, showing Tibs in uniform, proud as a peacock, with the new Mrs Burroughs resting, heavily pregnant, on his arm.

Poppy pinned the photograph up on the noticeboard and opened the letter from Sergeant Miller's mother. Mrs Miller would need to get over here soon, Poppy thought, for the sergeant had lost – and continued to lose – a considerable amount of blood. He was also in the early stages of septicaemia and, one by one, his major organs were failing.

She pulled out the card inside the envelope. It was black-edged with four printed words: *His will be done.* Handwritten, underneath, were the words *Norman Miller, RIP.*

Poppy opened the envelope wider and tapped it on the table, wondering if a sheet of notepaper had somehow got stuck inside, but there was nothing else. She went over to Sister and showed her the card.

'There was just this. No message, just Mrs Miller's name and address on the back of the envelope.'

'How very odd – and how shocking. The poor chap isn't even dead yet and she's RIP-ing him.'

'He asks a lot when his mother's coming . . .'

Sister nodded. 'I know. He asked me again just now when I was bandaging him.' She picked up the card. 'RIP – ripped in pieces, as the boys say. I'm afraid in his case it's most appropriate.'

'Perhaps his people are very religious – that's all I can think. Or perhaps they don't believe in medical intervention,' Poppy said.

'Not that we are intervening, because there's nothing that can be done for him, apart from keeping him comfortable.' Sister put the card in a drawer in her desk. 'I'll write to her again, emphasise that he hasn't got much time left and say he's asking for her.' She tutted. 'He's barely twenty, of course he's asking for his mother.'

Poppy picked up the letter with Matthews's address on the back. From the cardboard squareness of it, she thought it must contain a photograph of Billy's grave, and not feeling up to opening it right then, put it in her apron pocket to look at later.

Private Casey's parents had only been written to a few days before, but his mother arrived on a boat that afternoon and was at the hospital by two o'clock. She stood at Sister's desk, looking rather odd in a heavy winter overcoat, knitted scarf and old-fashioned hat with a feather. Sister, who was in the middle of a doctors' round, asked Poppy to take her over to see her son.

As they walked through the rows of beds, with Mrs Casey gasping and sighing at every turn about the numbers of men and the multitude of injuries, Poppy told her that her son's wound was healing well and there was no cause to be concerned just because she'd been invited over.

'Sister thought he could just do with a bit of a boost,' Poppy said. 'We often get a lad's parents over. It doesn't necessarily mean that there's anything very wrong.'

'My husband wanted to come as well, but there's the herd to look after and the milk to deliver,' said Mrs Casey.

'Of course.'

'And just between you and me . . . Are you Nurse Pearson?' Mrs Casey asked, looking at Poppy eagerly from under the brim of her hat.

Poppy nodded. 'Well, actually, I'm a VAD and not a nurse. But the boys call us all nurses.'

'Well, whatever you call yourself, Miss Pearson, I must tell you, my boy thinks the world of you. Writes about you all the time, he does: what you've said to him, what you've done.'

'Does he? That's nice,' Poppy said, wondering if it *was* nice.

'He says he gets special treatment from you . . . that you sit and talk to him in the afternoons and make him drinks when he gets upset.'

'Well, we do that for a lot of our boys,' Poppy said, wondering where this was all heading and fearing she knew. 'I try not to have favourites. Sister likes us to treat everyone the same.'

'Ah, but they're not all the same, are they?' Mrs Casey said, giving Poppy a look which was almost a wink, and Poppy began to feel rather uneasy.

On seeing her son, Mrs Casey burst into tears. Poppy gave her a handkerchief and went into the little kitchen to get her a cup of tea and give her time to settle herself. When she went back, Mrs Casey insisted that it should be Poppy who should sit down on the stool beside her son's bed. 'Do take the weight off your feet for a while. I know how hard you nurses work!'

Poppy, apprehensive now, sat down for a moment rather than cause a stir.

'Tell Nurse about our farm, Ma,' Private Casey said.

'Oh, it's a glorious spot. A hundred acres, we've got,' said his mother. 'And our own herd of Jersey cows.'

'How lovely,' Poppy said automatically.

'We've got a big farmhouse with lots of outbuildings, but you must see them for yourself. My husband and I were thinking that one of the barns could be converted into living accommodation.'

Poppy wasn't sure whether or not she'd heard right, or – if she had – what the woman could possibly mean. She stood up hastily, saying she must get on with the boys' tea, but that Mrs Casey was welcome to stay as long as she liked, and even take Private Casey out for a short walk if she wished. 'Anything he'd like to do, really,' Poppy added.

'Until he gets his ticket back home to England?'

Poppy shook her head. 'The news – the good news – is that your son's injury is quite a minor one and certainly not bad enough to get him sent home.'

'But you can help get him home, can't you? You can tell the doctors he's not well enough to fight – that he's a sensitive lad.'

'They wouldn't take any notice of me, I'm afraid,' Poppy said. 'I expect Private Casey will move on to convalesce for a couple of weeks and then, when he's quite well enough, will rejoin his regiment.'

'But I thought . . .'

Poppy busied herself tucking the sheet more tightly about Private Casey and brushing imaginary crumbs from the coverlet. 'Let Sister know if you want to go out for a walk,' she said briskly, 'and she'll ask one of the orderlies to help get him dressed.'

'And you'll come, too?'

'I'm afraid I wouldn't be able to do that,' Poppy said, panicking a little by then. 'I've too many other duties.'

'But surely they'll make an exception. I've come all the way from England to meet you – my son talks about you all the time.'

Poppy glanced at Private Casey, who was studying the counterpane intently. She shook her head. 'Mrs Casey, we have several boys on the ward who have their people over here visiting them, but we're not allowed to go out with them.' She gave a false laugh. 'Goodness, we'd never get our chores done if we were flitting about Boulogne all the time!'

Mrs Casey frowned at Poppy.

'If you like, I'm sure one of the orderlies would come out with you and show you around,' Poppy said.

'But I thought you and my son had an understanding. We don't want an orderly! If I speak to Sister and tell her that you and my son are —'

'Mother!' Private Casey suddenly interrupted, his face ruddy. 'I wrote and told you those things in secret. I said don't tell anyone else. I didn't know you were going to come over here.'

'Yes, yes,' said Mrs Casey, 'but a lad wants to know where he stands with a girl, doesn't he? And that lad's mother has a right to know, too.'

Poppy smiled, bright and efficient, but secretly horrified. 'If you don't mind me saying,' she said, 'I believe you've got the wrong end of the stick.'

Mrs Casey stared at her, affronted.

'Of course I enjoy talking to your son, Mrs Casey, but I've never been any more than his nurse — *one* of his nurses. If, somehow, he's got it into his head that I . . . Well, that's quite impossible. And now, if you'll excuse me, I really must get the boys' afternoon tea.'

Mortified, Poppy went into the kitchen and started laying up the trays for tea, crossly crashing the spoons and bread knives down so that one of the orderlies came up and asked who'd been ruffling her feathers.

How had *that* happened? She was perfectly sure that she hadn't, in any way, encouraged Private Casey. He was just a kid! But she would certainly tell Sister Gradley about this before anyone else did.

Later, at a quiet meeting with Sister, Poppy explained that somehow wires had got crossed.

'I don't know what Private Casey told his mother, or if it was her who got the wrong idea, but I think she only came over here to give me the once-over and decide if I'd make a suitable daughter-in-law. She was even talking about converting one of their farm buildings into a house for us!'

Sister frowned. 'And are you quite sure you –'

'Honestly, Sister! Not at all. I made a bit of a pet of him, but only because you asked me to. He's a nice lad, but – really!'

Sister shrugged. 'I'm afraid this sort of thing happens. Some of these young lads, homesick and frightened, haven't seen an English girl for several months, and when one shows any interest . . .' she put her hand up to ward off any protests from Poppy, 'even though it may be in the most innocent way, he thinks he's hit the jackpot. A pretty nurse of his own! What boy wouldn't like that?'

'What shall I do?' Poppy asked, relieved that Sister understood.

'Absolutely nothing. Be friendly, be professional, and wait for him to go back to his regiment – which he'll certainly have to do, because they're gathering up as many men as they possibly can.'

'The trouble is, he's just not cut out to be a soldier,' Poppy said.

'Our job is to patch him up and ship him out again,' Sister said. 'It's his regiment's job to make him into a soldier.'

'Yes, Sister Gradley.'

Poppy met Tilly and Dot in the canteen after work and was just about to tell them about Private Casey when she got a message saying that Sister wanted to see her.

'Would you mind sitting with Sergeant Miller for a couple of hours?' she asked when Poppy went back into Ward 5. 'He's very poorly indeed. One of the doctors has been down and says he's near the end. I'd stay myself, but I have an appointment with Matron and two majors – and the night staff don't know him like we do.'

'Of course I'll help,' said Poppy, saddened at the news, but pleased to be given the responsibility.

'I don't think he's got much longer,' Sister said, 'but if you're still at his bedside and it's past midnight, the night nurses will take over.'

Poppy dashed down to the canteen again and told Tilly and Dot she'd see them the following day, then went back to the ward. Mrs Casey was sitting by her son's bedside, knitting; the wave Poppy gave her wasn't returned.

Poppy put screens around Sergeant Miller's bed and pulled up a chair beside him.

Slowly, the daylight faded and several lanterns were lit, giving the ward a softer, kinder light. Mrs Casey went back to her guest house, patients settled themselves or asked for sleeping draughts, dozed fitfully or chatted to whoever was in the next bed. Some reread the latest letter they'd got from their sweethearts, holding up the pages in order to catch the nearest light.

Sergeant Miller, his breathing laboured and jagged, lay quite still. Sister had chosen not to tell him about the card from his mother, just that Mrs Miller hoped to be with him soon. For her part, Poppy found a cushion to sit on and a pile of socks to darn, and prepared herself for a long night.

Chapter Twenty-One

'other? Are you here, Ma?' Sergeant Miller
croaked.

'She'll be here soon,' Poppy said.

She had a sponge and a bowl of tepid water and she
wiped Sergeant Miller's forehead and sponged down
his arms to cool him. It was a stuffy, humid night, and
though the doors leading to the balcony were open,
there wasn't a trace of a breeze.

'Ma?' he said again, more faintly. 'Where are you?'

'She won't be long,' Poppy said, hoping that Mrs
Miller, wherever she was, had a decent excuse for not
being at her son's bedside when he was dying.

After a couple of hours, Poppy walked around the
ward to have a few words with the night staff and
stretch her legs. Her 'stroll' took her past Private
Casey's bed and, though from a distance she'd seen that
he was awake, when she tiptoed up to him, his eyelids
were shut tight.

'Private Casey,' she whispered. 'I'd like to speak to you for a moment.'

He didn't move.

'Private Casey,' she said again. 'I know you're awake.'

A moment went by and she looked anxiously across the ward towards Sergeant Miller's bed. How terrible if he died when she wasn't there! Imagine if Sister discovered that she'd been speaking to Private Casey at the time.

'Private Casey, I've allowed myself exactly one minute to speak to you.'

His eyes opened. 'You want to get back to the sergeant across the way, do you?' he said petulantly. 'Why are you still fussing over him?'

'Sergeant Miller is dying,' Poppy said in a low voice. 'If you were dying, you might hope that someone sat beside you in your final hours.'

Private Casey's expression didn't change. 'I thought you were bothered about me.'

'I was – I am,' Poppy said. 'I'm bothered about all our patients.'

'But me especially . . .'

'Look, you're a very nice boy,' Poppy said, 'but so are most of the boys in here. Sister said that if I had time I should come and talk to you and I was happy enough to do it, but I certainly didn't mean you to read anything into it. For one thing, we're not allowed to socialise with our patients in that sort of way.'

He didn't reply.

'You should never have told your mother that I was singling you out for special attention.'

There was a silence and Poppy glanced back to Sergeant Miller's bed once again.

'You want to go back over there, don't you?' Private Casey muttered.

'Yes, I do. It's my job and it's what Sister asked me to do.' Poppy could feel herself becoming irritated and tried to soften her next words. 'It's what nurses are here for – to give comfort. You wouldn't like to die alone, would you, with no one to hear your last words?'

There was another, longer silence, and then he mumbled, 'I expect you hate me now.'

'Of course I don't. I think you're a very nice boy who's rather out of place in the army.'

'I'm that, all right.'

'Well, there's a big offensive coming so perhaps that will fix things and the war will be over sooner than anyone thinks.' She managed to force a smile. 'And now I really must go back to my post. Goodnight, Private Casey.'

'G'night,' came the rather sullen reply.

It was half past eleven and Poppy, still at Sergeant Miller's bedside, had finished all the darning she'd brought with her and her eyes were aching with tiredness. Because of his severe stomach injury, her patient had had to stay on his back, but was now moving his legs constantly and restlessly, groaning as he tried to turn over and found himself unable to do so.

'Sergeant Miller, calm yourself,' Poppy kept saying, rather ineffectually. 'Try and rest.'

Another half-hour went by.

'Are you there, Ma?' he asked again and again, and Poppy, roundly cursing Mrs Miller, reassured him as much as she could.

The night sister came round and said there was no more that could be done for him, that he'd had all the pain relief they could give.

'Do you want to go to bed?' she asked Poppy. 'We can take over if you like.'

Poppy shook her head. 'I've been here so long I'd like to see the job through now. Thanks all the same.'

She thought about the letter from Matthews in her apron pocket. She'd been aware of its presence all day but, knowing what it must contain, had been putting off opening it. Now, nearing midnight and sitting beside a dying man, it seemed appropriate to look at a photograph of her brother's grave.

There were two pictures in the envelope. The first showed Billy's grave in a line with five other identical mounds of dark earth, each with a rough wooden cross at the top. The second was a close-up of Billy's own mound, the name *PRIVATE WILLIAM PEARSON* showing clearly on his cross. Someone, probably Matthews, had pressed a jam jar containing twists of pink honeysuckle into the earth.

Poppy started crying. How could she possibly send those to her mother? Suppose she hadn't even received the first letter telling her that he was dead?

The wheels at the bottom of the bed screen squealed as it was moved to one side, and one of the night orderlies appeared with a tray of mugs. 'Would you like some cocoa, dearie?'

Poppy thanked him and took a mug.

'Is that poor boy still with us?' said the orderly, an elderly chap, nodding towards Sergeant Miller.

'Yes, he is.'

The orderly dropped his voice. 'Having a hard time with him, are you?'

Poppy shook her head, dried her eyes. 'It's not him, exactly. I . . . I've just been looking at photographs of my brother's grave.'

'Ah,' said the orderly. 'Death everywhere you look. It's a sad old business, this war. But your brother's lucky to have a grave to rest in. Lots of boys are still out there in the mud and their bodies will never be found.'

'I know.'

'But we mustn't spend time on the dead. We must concentrate on helping the living, especially those boys who won't be here much longer.'

'Like Sergeant Miller here,' Poppy whispered.

'Like Sergeant Miller,' the man agreed. 'Help him to pass peacefully, dearie. Tell him what he wants to hear – lie if you have to – so that he can go in peace.'

He patted her hand and went out. Poppy drank her cocoa, thinking about what he'd said.

The next time Sergeant Miller asked restlessly for his ma, she replied, 'She's on her way, Sergeant. She's nearly here.'

Finishing her cocoa, Poppy put her candle lantern on to the floor, so that if her patient opened his eyes she would only appear as a silhouette.

Some minutes went by. 'Ma?' he asked. 'Are you here yet?'

Poppy took his hand in hers. 'Yes, I'm here,' she whispered.

His breath came out as a long sigh. 'At last. Will you kiss me goodnight, Ma?'

Poppy, trembling all over, leaned towards him and brushed his cheek with her lips.

'Ah . . .' was all he said, but the tension in his face disappeared, the muscles in his body began to relax and his limbs sank deeper into the mattress.

'Goodnight, son. God bless,' Poppy said.

His lips formed the word 'G'night' then he inhaled once more and breathed it out in a long sigh of relief. There were perhaps five more raggedy breaths, and then his personal war was over.

Poppy closed her eyes and said her own goodbye to him, then went to tell the night staff. She looked around for the old orderly who'd brought her the cocoa and advice, but there was no sign of him.

Ward 5,
Casino Hospital,
Nr Boulogne-sur-Mer,
France

15ᵗʰ June 1916

Dearest Ma,
I am very anxious because I haven't heard from you. I wrote just over a week ago to tell you about Billy's death, but have not had a word since. I'm worried that either you didn't get this letter, or I didn't get yours in reply. Please let me know if you would like me to send the photographs of Billy's grave? My friend Matthews sent them to me, and she has promised to keep the grave neat and tidy for us.

I hope Jane and Mary were not too upset at Billy's death. I'm afraid dying is a way of life over here – if that's not too odd a thing to say. Morale is still high, though, and we are all hoping that the next Big Push (whenever it happens) is the one which will decide things once and for all. We are not terribly busy at the moment, but it is the lull before the storm.

Dear Ma, I desperately want to hear from you. Please write back to me soon.
All my love,

Poppy x

Poppy sighed as she stuck down the envelope, wondering what to do if she still didn't hear anything. There were no other relatives alive now apart from old Aunt Ruby, and Ma wasn't living at home in Mayfield so she couldn't write to a neighbour to ask if they knew anything. Could she ask Miss Luttrell to investigate? Or, if the worst came to the very worst, ask for compassionate leave to go back to England for a few days? It was not a good time to ask for leave, however, seeing as the Push was coming. They were going to need every nurse and every VAD they could get.

'You'll never guess!' Dot said when the three girls had met up to take the air a day or so later. 'We have this cutie of a Tommy in our ward.' She turned to Tilly. 'Isn't that true? Isn't Norman Collier a stunner?'

'Absolutely a stunner!' Tilly confirmed.

'He put his name and address in one of your English papers, and sent in a photo, saying he was a lonely soldier in hospital with no one to write to, and what do you think?'

'I think he got lots of replies,' Poppy said.

'But guess how many!'

Poppy thought. 'Twenty? Fifty?'

'Three hundred and forty so far!' Dot squealed. 'They filled up three whole mail bags. The orderlies put them in piles all over the ward and our nursing sister went quite mad.'

'And they sent him presents, too: socks and ties, chocolate, ciggies and photographs!'

'And, oh my! You should see the photographs.'

'What were they like, then?' Poppy asked, intrigued.

'Well, I take back all I ever said about you Brits being quiet and reserved,' said Dot. 'These girls sure weren't.'

'So how did this gorgeous Norman Collier choose who to write to?' Poppy wanted to know.

'Well, he went through the photographs and picked out all the glamour girls – mostly wearing bathing costumes – then he let the unmarried boys in the ward choose whoever they wanted.'

'It kept them amused for two whole days while they sorted and swapped and bickered about the girls,' Tilly said.

'Say, talking of good-looking guys,' Dot said after a moment, 'we saw your doctor friend yesterday.'

'Oh?'

'You know who we mean, right?'

Poppy, nodding, said that she did.

'And he asked after you and wanted to send his best regards.'

'That's nice,' Poppy said.

Dot glanced at her. 'Hey, the girl has gone as red as her name!'

'That's because it's a warm day today,' said Poppy.

The letter, coming two days later, was in handwriting which Poppy didn't recognise, an old-fashioned, rounded script. Someone's mother writing to say how their boy was getting on now that he was home, Poppy thought as she opened it.

Bide-a-wee,
Logan,
Aberystwyth

26ᵗʰ June 1916

My dear Poppy,
I have hesitated some time before writing this letter, for I know how much you love being part of the war effort, and of course your help is so desperately needed in France. But you will have heard the expression 'charity begins at home' and I am afraid I need you to come back and look after your poor mother.

We received your first letter telling of Billy's sad death and then the second one, but your mother has not been able or inclined to answer either. This dreariness of spirit happened slowly and started some months back, before the news about your brother arrived. Since then, however, she has fallen into a melancholic state where she does very little except stare out of the window. Even your sisters cannot rouse her to show any interest in them or their welfare.

Your mother originally came to Wales to make her home here and care for me, but I fear I am now the one caring not only for her, but for your sisters, too. This I am now finding difficult, for I am rather frail physically and your sisters are robust, headstrong girls who take very little notice of me and my old-fashioned ways. The neighbours say that Mary especially is out of control.

Poppy, I am sorry to bring you such bad news, but we really cannot cope without you any longer. You must leave your nursing service and come back as quickly as you can.

With sincere wishes,

Aunt Ruby

Poppy, horrified, pushed the letter away from her. She wouldn't, couldn't bear the thought of going home! She'd pretend she'd never received Aunt Ruby's letter! She'd be like Tibs's Violet: if questioned, she'd say the letter must have got lost on the journey over. This was plausible, since mail ships were regularly getting torpedoed and their spoils sunk.

She was almost able to forget about the letter in the hurly-burly rush of the day, but when evening came and she walked out on to the sand dunes to try and clear her head, she started thinking about her mother. Nurses were supposed to be caring – and she did care. So how could she leave the four of them – her dearest ma, Aunt Ruby, Jane and Mary – all floundering? If they needed her then she had to go. Only, please, not quite yet . . .

Chapter Twenty-Two

Poppy took out the medical dictionary which held Freddie de Vere's wedding picture and tucked the photographs of Billy's grave inside the front cover. She put the book back in her locker and was about to go out when, on an impulse, she picked up the book again, took out the picture and stared at the bride and groom. She – pretty Miss Cardew, in her diamond tiara and silk gown – looked nothing but smug, she thought. And he, Freddie, looked trapped, caught as surely as a hare in a poacher's pocket.

Maybe he *had* loved her, but such a weak and watery love would never have been enough. He hadn't had the strength of mind, the ability, the manliness to oppose his mother. He'd fallen at the first hurdle.

Poppy screwed up the photograph and put it in the bin, and then threw away the letter from Aunt Ruby, too. She knew she would have to go home, but she couldn't think about it yet. She needed just a little more time. She wanted to be stationed in France for the Big Push – she wanted to be useful and valuable and brave. She also wanted to know if the interest that Michael Archer seemed to be showing her was real or just a wartime flirtation.

She tried to tell herself that it might not be so bad back in Blighty. Once she'd got things back to normal, got Ma some treatment for whatever malady she had and sorted out her sisters, then maybe she could enrol on a course to become a proper, qualified nurse. If not – well, there were hundreds of military hospitals in Britain, all of them doing valuable work. There was sure to be a hospital that needed volunteers close to where they were living, either in Wales with Aunt Ruby or back in Mayfield.

If Aunt Ruby wrote again, Poppy decided, then that meant it really was urgent and she'd start arranging to go back right away. If no second letter came, then it might mean, perhaps, that Aunt was able to cope on her own for a little longer. She *would* return and help out at home, of course, but would leave it as long as she dared, perhaps making the excuse to Aunt Ruby that she had to give a month's notice.

The wards of the Casino Hospital and all the other base hospitals continued to be cleared of as many patients as possible. Most of them – including Private Casey – went on to convalescent homes, while others went back to England a little earlier than they would have done normally.

Waving goodbye from the balcony to a small group of Ward 5 boys, Poppy saw a group of nine men, led by an orderly, proceeding in single file along the dusty road to the docks. Each man except the orderly at the front had been blinded, and each had his right hand on the shoulder of the man in front. In this way, singing *Take Me Back to Dear Old Blighty*, they trekked towards the ship which would take them home.

One night at the end of June, all the medical staff of the hospitals in and around Boulogne who weren't on duty, as well as recovering patients and local dignitaries, were invited to a 'Grand Music Hall'. This was a morale-boosting exercise to be held in the old Hôtel de Ville in Boulogne.

When the nurses arrived at the old city hall at seven o'clock, spruce in clean aprons, some daringly wearing a smear of pink lip balm, most of them were disappointed to find that nurses and VADs were to be seated alongside their respective ward sisters and matrons, and apart from the male medical staff.

There was some low-key muttering and grumbling about this, and the girls were moving rather reluctantly towards their seats, when a much-decorated general in dress uniform appeared on the stage.

'If Matron-in-Charge is willing,' he said, 'I propose that men and women should be allowed to sit together, just as they would at home.' A cheer went up from the boys. 'After all, I'm sure we can be trusted to behave like gentlemen for a couple of hours.'

'Norman Collier can't!' some wag called, for the tale of the good-looking Tommy and his fan mail had spread throughout the Boulogne hospitals.

As the laughter faded away, Poppy and the rest of the VADs looked anxiously towards Matron-in-Charge, whose expression hadn't altered. The general went over to her, they exchanged a few words and, to another rousing cheer, he kissed her hand. He went back on the stage to say that Matron-in-Charge had graciously agreed to allow both sexes to sit together.

There followed a scramble by the young men, while the girls tried to look slightly bemused, as if they didn't care one way or another. Poppy, wondering what to do if no one came and sat beside her, suddenly became aware that Michael Archer was leaping over the seats like a deer in order to reach her quickly.

'Phew!' he said, claiming the seat beside her. 'It's a good job I've been in training for this.'

The Push was the number one topic for almost everyone there, but after that Poppy told him the story of the mysterious orderly who, when she'd been sitting beside a dying man, had come into the ward dispensing cocoa and thoughtful advice.

'And the funny thing is,' she concluded, 'the night staff didn't even see him at all.'

'Ah,' said Michael. 'He sounds like a ghost to me.'

Poppy laughed. 'Do you really think so?'

'I think we could quite reasonably start a rumour about it.'

'But there's no such thing!' Poppy said, thinking of the Grey Lady of Netley.

'That's as maybe, but everyone loves spooky stories,' he said, 'especially if the ghosts encountered are spiritually enlightened ones. Let's push the rumour out there and see how quickly it gets back to us. Winner gets a . . .' He raised his eyebrows. 'Well, we can decide on that later.'

Poppy laughingly agreed.

'You must promise to pass on the story at least twice a day.'

'I promise.'

'And I do, too,' he said, turning to her and saying the words so solemnly, it was as if he was vowing something quite different.

The music hall turns started. There were jugglers, men who climbed on each other's backs to form pyramids, a dog that could add up, and lots of singers, including the Little Orphan and the Henpecked Man, who both came with accompanying songs. The finale that evening was everyone's favourite, the Soldier Far from Home. This was a regular infantryman sitting in a tent on the stage, writing letters home to recipients who magically appeared before him. His act included such well-known songs as 'There's a Long, Long Trail A-winding' and 'Keep the Home Fires Burning'. By the time he got to 'If You Were the Only Girl in the World', there wasn't a dry eye in the house.

At this point, Poppy became aware of the warmth of Michael Archer's arm on the seat rest beside hers, touching her arm all the way down from shoulder to elbow. Did he really like her, she wondered, or was he just being friendly because they were both far from home? But, even if he really was attracted to her, how could it come to anything once she was back in England? What was the point of falling in love when there was a war on?

During the nights following the 'Grand Music Hall', there was a heavy bombardment of an area to the south, somewhere (so rumour had it) around the River Somme. It lit up the sky in an astonishing display of noisy fireworks and prevented Poppy and nearly everyone else from sleeping. It went on for several days and nights, and someone in the canteen told Poppy that the Allies were trying to shell through the masses of barbed wire protecting the German trenches, thus giving the infantry a chance to gain ground.

Going out one morning on an errand for Sister, Poppy was surprised to see that a huge marquee had been erected on a scruffy piece of land behind the Casino and, going closer, saw piles of iron bedsteads waiting to be erected, and several carts full of what looked like mattresses and pillows.

'Yes, the hospital expects a very large number of new patients,' Sister explained to Ward 5 staff later.

Poppy shared a look with one of the other VADs – a look of alarm.

'Are there going to be that many?' the VAD asked.

Sister nodded. 'I'm afraid the whole hospital is going to be frightfully busy. The Push has most definitely begun.'

The next afternoon, the casualties began arriving. Having already filled up the hospitals close to the fighting, they were being transported further and further across country in order to find empty beds.

When it was Ward 5's turn, Sister took a team of nurses, VADs and orderlies down to the railway station. The orderlies carried back the most badly wounded on stretchers; others in bath chairs were pushed by nurses. The walking wounded were helped along by those working nearby – shop assistants, laundry workers, drivers – anyone who had an hour or two to spare and wanted to help.

Poppy brought back Private Cassidy, a man who'd lost his foot to a grenade.

'That's my lot,' he said chirpily, limping along with one arm around Poppy's neck. 'I reckon it was almost worth losing a foot to get out of it.'

'Really?' Poppy asked in disbelief. 'Was it that terrible?'

'That first day,' he said, shaking his head, 'it was like the whole world had gone mad. I never want to be part of anything like . . .' He suddenly gave a shout of pain and doubled up, and it was some time before he could speak.

He leaned against the wall for several moments, his face white. When they set off again, it was very slowly.

'I had an easy time of it compared to some,' he said. 'Just think – one hit and that's the end of my army career. I'll get an injury stripe on my uniform and see out the rest of the war at home. How's that for good fortune?'

'Not everyone would agree with you . . .'

'Yeah, but the way I look at it, it could have taken me head off instead of me foot, couldn't it?'

'It could,' Poppy agreed.

'And me missus'll be right pleased to have me home.'

'Of course,' Poppy said, biting her lip. Since her aunt's letter, any mention of home evoked feelings of guilt in her. She'd decided, however, that she'd get through the Push, then tell Sister about the letter from Aunt Ruby and ask her advice.

She hadn't been able to see much of Dot and Tilly lately, for their hospital was also taking in scores of new casualties and, as qualified nurses, they were allowed to do a much greater variety of work than Poppy was, including assisting with operations. Both had now applied to work

226

at a casualty clearing station, telling Poppy that it was the most vital, exciting and terrifying work a girl could possibly imagine.

As they passed each other in the canteen that evening, Dot asked Poppy if she'd heard about the mysterious disappearing man. Poppy, not knowing what she was about to hear, said she hadn't.

'Well, he just came out of nowhere into a ward one night,' Dot continued. 'He told the nurse he'd come to collect someone who was dying.'

'He was an old, old man with a long beard and a grey cloak,' added Tilly.

'Like the Grim Reaper?' Poppy asked, now realising where the story was going. 'Did he have a scythe?'

'Probably,' Dot said.

'Let's say yes,' said Tilly.

'Anyway, he appeared out of nowhere and said these incredibly wise words about life and death and so on,' Dot went on. 'He told the nurse she should allow her patient to let go of life, so she did and he died. And when she looked for the old man to thank him for his advice, he'd disappeared.'

'No one in the whole hospital ever saw him again!' Tilly added dramatically.

'Really?' Poppy bit her lip to stop herself laughing.

'They're saying that in ancient times a hospital stood here, and the wise old man is a ghost doctor from those times,' Dot said.

'Do you think it's really true?' Tilly asked.

Poppy was unable to stop herself laughing any longer.

'What?' both girls said.

'There's something I have to tell you,' said Poppy. 'I hope you're not going to be too disappointed . . .'

That evening Poppy wrote to Matthews.

Casino Hospital,
Nr Boulogne-sur-Mer

3rd July 1916

Dearest Matthews,
Thank you for looking after me so well and thanks also to your Stanley for sending me the photographs. I am so grateful to you for making such a horrid task a little easier to bear and I'm sorry not to have written and thanked you before. Stanley sounds like a lovely chap and I know you will be blissfully happy together, even if you decide to leave the wedding until the war is over.

I have not sent the photographs to my ma yet. I wrote twice to tell her about Billy, but have only had back a letter from my aunt, who says Ma has some sort of nervous trouble and hardly ever speaks. And my sisters seem to be running wild.

I really don't know what to do. Aunt wants me home because she says she can't cope any longer, so I think I'll have to go – but how awful it will be to leave. I know it's quite dreadful of me, but I don't want to go, and I can't tell Dot and Tilly or anyone. Only you! Matthews, what on earth can I do?

I must cut this short, as Sister has just sent a message asking me to go to Matron's office as a matter of urgency. I am already feeling quite ill with terror wondering what it is that I've done wrong.

Fondest love,

Pearson x x x

Chapter Twenty-Three

P oppy had no idea what Sister could want – let alone Matron. She'd only glimpsed that esteemed person a few times and had certainly never spoken to her.

With Matron, or any other high-up War Office being, she knew that you only spoke when spoken to, but other than that had no idea of the etiquette that might be involved in such a meeting.

What could this possibly be about? Waiting in the anteroom to Matron's office, Poppy scoured her mind for possible violations of the many regulations.

Had someone seen her enjoying herself with Dot and Tilly? Had she misbehaved, laughed too immodestly, at the concert hall the other night? Had the picnic in the woods been reported to someone in authority?

Suddenly she thought of something far worse: suppose Aunt Ruby had written to Devonshire House demanding that Poppy return to England immediately?

Poppy was called into an inner room, a spartan little office, where Matron sat with Sister Gradley. Sister introduced Poppy to Matron, who shook her hand and asked her to take a seat.

The two of them seemed very serious, Poppy thought, but not especially grim. It did not appear that she was about to be told off for breaking some rule or other.

'Pearson, you've been recommended for a special task,' Matron said. 'At another time we would have called on a qualified nurse, but with the multitude of casualties expected over the next few days now that the offensive has started, we can't afford to let one go.'

Poppy waited. Now was the time, she thought, to confess that she was needed at home, say she was terribly sorry but she couldn't do whatever it was they wanted her to do.

On the other hand, surely she ought to hear Matron out? Perhaps it was something she could do quickly, one last special task that would go down on her record and make it easier to find a job in a hospital when she got home.

'We can ill afford to lose any of our VADs, either, but I know you to be sensible and able to use your initiative,' Sister said with a slight smile.

'As you will have deduced,' Matron went on, 'we are at the beginning of what could prove a long and difficult battle, centred around the area known as the Somme.'

Poppy nodded.

'A situation has occurred in this area.' Matron and Sister exchanged glances. 'A young man – we're calling him Patient X – has been badly injured and also has respiratory trouble because of poisonous gas, so we need to get him out of the clearing station he's in as quickly as possible. The War Office has asked us to provide a nursing assistant who will accompany a doctor to that area and help bring him out.'

'You won't be responsible for the patient's safety or involved in any decisions about his well-being,' Sister said. 'It's just a case of bedpans, bandages and doing whatever you can to aid whoever will be looking after him on the journey.'

'This is not a particularly dangerous mission as you should be well away from the fighting,' said Matron. 'But it is a confidential and important one. If the enemy knew there was someone we badly wanted to bring out, then they'd do everything they could to thwart us.'

Poppy nodded, rather excited.

'Have you any questions?' Matron finished.

Poppy hesitated, then asked, 'Why him? Why is he so important?'

'Well, firstly, X-rays show that he's got a piece of shrapnel lodged near his brain, so he needs a very delicate operation that only a specialist surgeon in England would be able to tackle,' Matron said. 'The other reason is that he's the son of a military man – one of our most important and well-known generals – who's already lost two boys in this war. Patient X is his final, youngest son, and if anything can be done to get him out and save his life then we've pledged to do it.' She went on to say that Poppy would depart Boulogne on the 6.00 a.m. train the following morning and should be back before nightfall. The doctor she'd be accompanying had all the official papers and would be at the ticket office at a quarter to the hour.

Sister said that she hoped Poppy realised the honour of being given such a task. 'You will, of course, act with decorum at all times,' she said. 'Remember you are a representative of the British Army. If you let your standards slip, even for a moment, then you risk bringing the whole nursing profession into disrepute.'

'There are still some men who seem to think that we shouldn't even be over here,' Matron added.

'Yes, Matron, Sister.'

'You'll be under the command of the doctor you'll be accompanying at all times, of course,' Sister said. 'You already know that VADs are not normally allowed on clearing stations or anywhere near the front line, so you must be self-effacing to the point of fading into the background.'

Poppy nodded and promised to work to the best of her ability.

Later, still wondering if she should have taken the job, she concluded that she couldn't have done anything else. To be given the honour of undertaking such a task and then to turn round and say that she couldn't do it . . . Well, it would have been most dreadfully disrespectful.

She asked one of the orderlies to wake her early, then went to her room and packed a clean apron and a few other things in a canvas bag.

She considered adding a PS to the letter to Matthews telling her why she'd been summoned to Matron, then decided she ought not, in case she got into trouble with the censor.

It was nearly midnight. She laid out her uniform on the back of her chair and tried to sleep.

Sleep, however, didn't arrive. She thought about her mother and her sisters, about the job she'd been given to do, and about how pleasing it was that she could think about Freddie de Vere on his wedding day without bursting into tears. She also thought a little about Michael Archer, wondering if their relationship was leading anywhere. He was such a joker – how was a girl supposed to tell if he was serious? She'd already been fooled by Freddie . . .

Two hours later, still unable to sleep because of the uncomfortable, miserable feeling that she'd abandoned her mother and sisters, she decided what she must do. She relit her candle and found a notepaper and envelope.

Casino Hospital,
Nr Boulogne-sur-Mer,
France

8ᵗʰ July 1916

Dear Aunt Ruby,
I am so sorry I haven't replied to your letter before. To tell you the absolute truth, I've been rather dreading having to write, because I knew that when I did it would set everything in motion and I'd be obliged to come home. That makes me sound callous, but I really hope you don't think I am. It's just that a VAD's work here is so valuable and engrossing it will be hard to leave it.

Ma comes first, of course, and I'm very concerned about her, so when I return tonight from an errand I intend to tell Sister that I'm needed at home and will ask to be released from my contract. I shall stress that it's urgent and hope to be with you as soon as possible.

Aunt Ruby, kindly tell my sisters that they'll have me to reckon with if they misbehave, and do please reassure Ma that I will soon – very soon – be home.

Much love,

Poppy x

Having done this, she was finally able to sleep.

When the orderly came to wake Poppy at five o'clock the next morning, it was light outside. Quickly getting dressed, she left a note in Dot's pigeonhole saying she was probably going to be out all day, and posted the letters to Matthews and her aunt. The hospital canteen was not yet open, so the hot drink and roll that Poppy had been looking forward to didn't materialise. Perhaps she'd be able to get something on the train, she thought, remembering the day she and Matthews, as trainee VADs, had buttered hundreds of rolls on a troop train going up-country from Southampton.

At Boulogne station Poppy found herself in an absolute sea of khaki. Hundreds – thousands – of soldiers were milling about, in their platoons or in smaller groups, coming and going to and from the front line, carrying kitbags almost as big as themselves. There were nurses to be seen in all-shades-of-blue dresses, a brass band was playing, and it looked very much as if a hospital train was expected in, because a whole team of orderlies carrying rolled-up stretchers was moving towards one of the platforms.

Poppy could see the main ticket office ahead of her but, being early, decided she'd try and get to the café to buy a cup of tea and something to eat. The Red Cross snack bar at Boulogne station was rough and ready, made out of two old railway trucks and a pile of wooden pallets, but hugely popular with not only Tommies but the French and Belgian soldiers who passed through the station day and night and always wanted cocoa and buns. There was a baker in Boulogne who turned out hundreds of these sugared confections every day of the week, the ingredients (currants, raisins, cherries) depending on what was available.

Poppy hesitated, rather unwilling to push herself into the scrum of boys.

However, someone noticed her and called, 'VAD coming!' and, 'Let the little lady through!'

The sea of khaki parted for her as if by magic. Rather pink in the face, Poppy found herself at the front of the café queue, ordered what she wanted and managed to find a quiet corner away from everyone, where she ate her bun as tidily as possible.

Ten minutes later, she was ready and waiting at the ticket office. She hoped very much that the doctor she'd be helping would be reasonably pleasant. She knew that some of the older doctors were very important army men – that is, they were army generals before they were doctors, and might think themselves a bit above travelling with a VAD.

'Pearson!'

She wheeled around. 'Oh! Doctor Archer – Michael,' she said, surprised and rather pleased to see him. 'What are you doing here?'

He smiled. 'The same as you.'

'What?'

'We're going together to a casualty clearing station to collect Patient X.'

'No!'

'I rather think yes.' He brushed the tip of her nose with his finger. 'Excuse me, but you have sugar on your nose. Did you leave it there in order to look endearing?'

Poppy tried not to smile – and failed.

Chapter Twenty-Four

Poppy and Michael Archer waited, yawning, on the platform for the train which was going to take them to the casualty clearing station.

'But how did you . . . I mean, why are you going?' Poppy asked. 'Why you and not anyone else?' What she really wanted to know was if Michael had had any choice in his travelling companion. Whether he had, in fact, asked for her.

'Why me?' He shrugged. 'Probably the same reason as "Why you?". Because we're both newly qualified and good enough to be sent, but not so good that they'll miss us too much when we're not at our hospitals.'

'So it was just the luck of the draw?'

'Exactly. Did I know about you beforehand? No. Did I give three cheers when I looked at the paperwork last night and found out? Yes.'

Poppy smiled, thinking that there was something about him that was fair and uncomplicated and honest.

She didn't have to put on airs with him or pretend to be any different than the way she really was. And, best of all, he made her laugh.

'Do you believe in fate, Pearson?'

Poppy frowned. 'I don't know. Sometimes ... perhaps ...'

'Well, I don't know, either, but it is a bit funny the way we keep bumping into each other in wards and markets and on picnics, isn't it?'

'Mmmm,' Poppy murmured, not wanting to commit herself one way or the other.

'Just think, they could have settled on any VAD to accompany any doc on this trip, but they picked me, and then they picked you, and here we both are.' He grinned. 'What d'you think? Isn't that fate?'

'I don't know,' Poppy said after a moment's thought, 'but I do know that I still don't believe in ghosts.' And she told him how Dot and Tilly had related the tale of the Mysterious Bedside Visitor, who had become considerably more mysterious with each telling and now had a cloak, beard and possibly also a scythe.

Michael admitted that no one had actually come back to him with the story, so they declared Poppy the winner and Michael said that he would treat her to tea and a bun when they reached Boulogne station on the way home.

They waited while an extremely long train puffed into the station and disgorged walking-wounded casualties, equipment, stores, newspapers and even horses on to their platform. Once it had emptied, it took them ten minutes or so to find their seats and more than half an hour before the train was ready to move off again. Their carriage held eight people, and Poppy, as the only female, enjoyed being deferred to regarding whether or not the window should be open or closed and if she wanted to sit in direct sunlight. The boys in the carriage also modulated their language around her and were careful that cigarette smoke did not waft in her direction.

When the train started, no one seemed to know which route it was taking or which towns or villages it would pass through.

'Security, I suppose,' Michael said. 'The fewer people that know where a valuable commodity like a train is going, the better.'

'Half the time even the driver doesn't know the route,' someone in the carriage said. 'He gets his instructions on the way.'

They stopped several times, including at a siding to pick up some lightly injured casualties who were going back to join their regiment. Close by here, Poppy saw four newly dug graves by the side of the track.

Whispering, she pointed them out to Michael, and he said they were probably casualties who'd died on one of the hospital trains coming back from the front line. 'Yesterday or perhaps the day before,' he added.

'But couldn't the authorities have waited until they got to Boulogne and buried them there in a proper cemetery?'

He shook his head. 'The last thing anyone would want to do is travel with a clutch of dead bodies,' he said. 'Imagine in the hot weather . . .'

'Oh, of course not.'

'It would be depressing for those who'd survived to travel among corpses, and disheartening for the hospital staff who'd have to take them off at the other end.'

Poppy nodded. She began to take more notice of what was outside and saw several more little mounds and crosses beside the railway line. 'It's so sad to think that these boys survived the battle, but couldn't take the journey.'

'Exactly,' said Michael. 'If they could have been operated on in a field hospital, they might have lived.'

'Then why weren't they?'

'Quite simply, there have been far too many casualties. Even with double the number of tented operating rooms and treble the number of doctors, they still couldn't have coped with the numbers coming in these past few days.'

Michael and Poppy should have been at their destination by ten o'clock, but the train came to a complete halt after Albert station, and no information was forthcoming about when it might move again. Passengers got up, stretched their legs, even left the train to walk around outside.

In the distance – but not so far in the distance as Poppy might have liked – the guns could be heard, a constant rattle and boom, as smoke rose in dark, menacing whorls and mingled with the clouds. *Boys dying everywhere*, Poppy thought dismally, *friends and enemies*. Every bang and boom meant another death – or ten, or forty. The war was like some fiendish machine demanding a constant supply of dead bodies to keep it going.

The heat, her early start and the fact that she'd barely slept the night before all made Poppy feel weary, and to try and stay awake she suggested a game of I Spy. The next thing she knew was waking up to find the train moving again and her head on Michael's shoulder.

'Oh!' she exclaimed, sitting up straight. 'I'm so sorry.' Imagine – oh, imagine if a sister or a senior officer had seen her!

He looked at her quizzically. 'That was the biggest cheat ever.'

'What was?' she asked, embarrassed.

'You asked me to play I Spy, gave me the impossible letter Y and then fell asleep so I couldn't play.'

Poppy laughed. 'I don't even remember what I thought of now.' She looked around the carriage. 'Where did everyone go?' she asked. Apart from them, the carriage now held only one sleeping soldier.

'We stopped at a couple of places while you were fast asleep. God knows where we are now, though.' He stood up, looked out of the window and up and down the line.

'Not that I don't enjoy being with you, but I'm thinking about our patient. Bad lungs, possible trench fever and a piece of shrapnel lodged near the brain are not a good combination to keep waiting.'

Poppy stared out into acres of countryside, worried about the patient they had to care for and also wondering how vulnerable they were to fire from enemy aircraft. This time, there were no big red crosses on the top of their carriages to help keep them safe.

'We'll be coming back on a hospital train, won't we?' she asked.

'Definitely,' Michael replied. 'Patient X's head will be in a holding device – he has to be kept flat and still.' He glanced at Poppy. 'That'll be your job.'

Poppy nodded.

'We make a good team, eh?'

'We haven't done anything yet!' Poppy said. He really was, she thought, awfully nice.

Another half-hour went by. The train stopped for ten minutes, and when it started again it went backwards.

'We seem to be going off on a branch line,' Michael said.

'How can it go backwards?'

'There's an engine at each end,' Michael said. 'Didn't you see them when we got on?'

Poppy shook her head. 'Can I tell you something?' she asked abruptly.

When he said that of course she could, she told him that she'd not heard from her mother since she'd written to tell her about Billy, and then continued with the rest of the story about Aunt Ruby and her sisters. Hardly knowing why she'd suddenly felt compelled to tell him, she finished, 'Oh, but I really don't want to go home!'

Michael nodded slowly, as if weighing things up. 'But you must.'

'Yes . . .'

'And you *are* going, aren't you?'

Her eyes filled with tears. 'I wrote to my aunt to tell her so this morning.'

'Of course you must go to your family. That's the sort of girl you are.'

He squeezed her hand and, as she turned to smile at him, there came the certain knowledge that, if it hadn't been for the remaining chap in their carriage, he would have kissed her. What was more, she would have kissed him back.

When they finally arrived at the massive tented clearing station, Poppy discovered why it was that every nurse said they wanted the experience of working at one, for here was a bewildering, electrifying maelstrom of activity. There was a vast laundry where miles of clean muslin bandages fluttered on washing lines, and scores of small and large tents where patients were either operated on or made ready to move on to a more permanent place at a base hospital. Ambulances and

Red Cross trucks were all over the place, while nurses and white-clad doctors scuttled everywhere, busy as ants. In far greater numbers, however, were the wounded. Hundreds of them, everywhere one looked, were being hurried along by stretcher-bearers, with injured faces covered, with limbs missing; some men screaming and with such horrendous wounds that Poppy could hardly bear to see them. They also passed a line of blind men, with stained bandages around their eyes, sitting with their backs against a wall as if scared to move from there. Nearly every casualty was caked in mud, weary, disillusioned or tearful.

'Oh, God,' Poppy whispered.

'This is what hell must be like,' Michael said quietly.

He went off to try and discover the whereabouts of Patient X, while Poppy waited at the entrance to what she presumed was the mess tent and tried to keep out of everyone's way. Looking at the half-cleared trestle tables within the tent, she could see several plates of food hardly started, abandoned by those who'd been called away to an emergency.

'Just arrived, have you?' a passing stretcher-bearer asked. Seeing her staring in, he went on, 'The doctors don't get no time to eat, see. They get a break and rush in here, then get called back again before they're done.'

'It all seems quite . . . unbelievable,' Poppy said, indicating their surroundings.

'Yesterday was worse,' the bearer said. He was plump, in his mid-forties, and sweating badly. 'We brought in

246

wave after wave of 'em, lined 'em up on stretchers right round the camp, until the medics said they couldn't take no more. Awful bad, they were. On the brink of death, many of 'em. Stomachs ripped open, chests caved in, faces gone.'

'How terrible . . .'

'But if they's still breathing, see, they's got a chance of pullin' through. It's them that disappears that gets to me.' He shook his head as if having difficulty putting the concept into words. 'Like, they're here one minute, gawn the next. Not a trace left. They've been blown to smithereens, see. Disappeared into the air. Not even a fingernail left of 'em.'

Poppy bit her lip hard and stared at him, wanting very badly for him to stop telling her about it.

'They're saying that thousands got killed on the first day of fighting, ain't they? Where did they all go, then? We got lots to bury, but not thousands like they say we've lost.'

Poppy gazed at him mutely.

'Blown to bits, they was! It don't bear thinking about, do it?'

Poppy was thinking that she'd have to be rude and just walk away, when there came a bellow from a tent of 'Stretcher-bearer!'.

The man touched his forehead and winked. 'Duty calls, Nurse! But I've enjoyed our chat.'

Poppy stood still, eyes brimming. Now she understood why the War Office didn't allow VADs to work at clearing stations. Hearing, seeing, smelling, walking with Death every day would be just too much for all but the most sensible, the most experienced of nurses with the strongest constitutions.

She stood waiting, watching, for twenty minutes or so, aghast and incredulous by turns. She could see why they called it the 'Theatre of War', for the sloping field before her was like a giant stage on which the actors – the men and women, nurses, soldiers and orderlies, – all had their vital parts to play.

Once she glimpsed Michael in the distance, where the hospital tents were on rising ground, hurrying behind a man, perhaps a surgeon, who was wearing a white cotton gown stained with blood.

When he eventually came back, his face was pale and his silver-grey eyes were clouded.

'What is it?' Poppy asked fearfully.

He took a breath. 'I'm afraid our patient is dead. He died two hours ago, while we were still getting here.'

Poppy stared at him, then burst into tears. Amid so much death and so much sorrow, she knew it was absurd to single out one young man to cry about, a boy she didn't even know, but she couldn't help herself. She'd really wanted this nameless, injured, important boy – who might be her last patient – to be saved.

At three o'clock, Poppy was sitting with Michael on a pile of sacks by the gates of the clearing station. From here, they could see the small railway station with its tracks going off in both directions. The pair of them looked, and felt, drained and utterly despondent.

'I thought that if I could bring him out, I would have helped something really good to happen,' Michael said.

Poppy nodded miserably. 'I thought that, too. One last deed before I went home.'

'He was a young officer – nineteen, I think. His two older brothers are already dead.'

'I know.' Poppy's instinct was to place her head on Michael Archer's shoulder, but she couldn't do that, so she leaned against him a little, trying to be of comfort without looking as if she was. 'First his two older brothers, and then him. His parents must be . . . Oh, it's just not fair! Perhaps if we'd got here earlier . . .'

'I was told that the train we caught this morning was the first one.' Michael sighed and looked at his watch. 'Did they say three-fifteen for the train back to Albert?'

Poppy nodded. 'Change there for Boulogne,' she said, her voice croaky with tiredness.

'Nothing coming yet – in either direction,' Michael said, looking up the lines. 'Funny how no one else is here, waiting for it.'

The sun was hot and Poppy was so tired that she closed her eyes. After a moment, her head drooped, making her start and wake up again suddenly.

Michael gave her a small smile. 'I obviously have so much charisma that as soon as we're alone, you fall asleep.'

Poppy stretched her eyes open, trying to wake herself. 'Perhaps it's just that I feel safe with you.'

He darted a look at her, surprised, smiling, and Poppy became embarrassed by the message her words must have conveyed. She was about to try and explain what she'd meant (and probably, she thought, get in more of a muddle), when an army doctor, kneeling beside a stretcher on the ground some distance off, called, 'Nurse! Over here, please!'

'I'm not a –' Poppy began.

'Nurse!' he said, more urgently.

She looked at Michael, who shrugged.

'Your choice,' he said.

Poppy jumped up and ran over to help.

'He's haemorrhaging!' The doctor shoved a clean wad of gauze and flannel at Poppy. 'Just apply pressure on that wound.'

The soldier lying on the ground – just one of a line of unconscious casualties on stretchers, waiting to be seen and operated on – appeared to have been slashed in the groin by a bayonet. He was unconscious, with blood pumping out from a deep wound at the top of his thigh.

'Press as hard as you can,' the field doctor said. 'I'm going to run up to the mess tent and get a couple of stretcher-bearers. This fella needs to jump the queue.'

'I'll give you a hand,' Michael said. 'We can take him ourselves.'

With Poppy walking beside them and maintaining the pressure on the wound, the two doctors carried the unconscious patient to the nearest operating theatre and handed him over to the surgical team.

Michael went over to speak to a medic he recognised and came back to where Poppy was waiting, looking grim. 'The doctors are saying they've never seen so many casualties from one source,' he said. 'They're operating day and night – mostly amputations – and they still can't keep up.'

'And what about out there? Are we winning? Are we gaining ground?'

'No one's saying, but I can see from their faces . . .' He looked away and struggled to compose himself. 'Apparently our artillery bombed the German lines for several days in order to cut through the barbed-wire barricades and give our lads a chance of reaching the enemy lines, but it didn't work. When the boys came out of their trenches and started towards the German lines, they got tangled up in great snarls of wire.' His voice cracked. 'They became sitting targets.' He shook his head, too choked with emotion to say any more.

A padre called over to ask them to help take cups of water around to patients in one of the tents. By the time they'd done this, they'd either missed the train they were meant to take to Albert or it had never arrived. There being no later train stopping at the clearing station that day, they were advised by an official to walk to a siding two miles or so ahead, where a train for Boulogne was due to make a brief halt at six o'clock that evening.

As they set off, Poppy thought how very odd it was that at home in England, before the war, she'd hardly been on her own with a boy, let alone ever spoken to one as freely as she could speak to Michael. How much things had changed in just two years.

They were both exhausted by the time they reached the siding, which was no more than a short curve of extra line alongside the main one. Within the curve was an ugly bunker containing sandbags and piles of rubble, and Poppy went in to try and find shelter from the sun.

'I'm so tired I could sleep standing up,' Poppy said. 'I hardly slept at all last night.'

'Nor did I.' He yawned widely, apologised for it, then said, 'You first, then.'

'Me first what?'

'To say what it was that was keeping you awake.'

'I couldn't possibly.'

'Oh, please do. I'm terribly curious – and anyway, we're both so tired I'm sure we won't remember anything in the morning.'

'All right,' Poppy said after a moment. 'I was thinking mostly about my mother, my sisters, my life as a VAD and my . . . my ex-sweetheart.'

'Really? Your ex-sweetheart?' He looked intrigued. 'Who was that, then?'

'Oh, just someone I knew when I was at Netley,' Poppy said.

'And you didn't think about anyone else at all?'

Poppy shook her head. 'No one,' she said innocently, knowing exactly what he was getting at. 'Who else would there be?'

'I wonder.'

'Now it's your turn. What . . . who . . . were you thinking of?'

'You.'

The word came out in such a matter-of-fact way that Poppy wasn't sure if she'd heard it correctly.

'You,' he repeated. 'It's always you that I think about. Ever since that moment in Netley where you mistook me for an orderly.'

'Oh.'

'Always you . . .'

For a moment they stared at each other, both of them amazed and thrilled, and then Poppy took a step towards him and tripped on a rock. She would have fallen, but he put out his arms, caught her and held her tightly to him.

Chapter Twenty-Five

No train came along that evening. At least, none that stopped at the siding. There was a train that steamed along when the last of the daylight was fading, sometime around ten o'clock, but Michael, who'd been asleep, didn't hear it until it had almost gone by and it was too late to hail it. Besides, it was full of casualties going to base hospitals and there would have been hundreds of injured men crammed into every corner.

Poppy, too, was asleep by then, curled up on concrete sandbags, emotionally drained and so weary that she slept despite the heavy bombing just a few miles away. She managed to sleep a little more on the train which stopped to pick them up at first light the next morning and conveyed them slowly, joltingly, back to Boulogne.

When she woke properly, she found Michael very quiet, and couldn't help wondering if he was regretting the things he'd said to her the evening before. Maybe he'd just been moved to speak because of the raw, traumatic day they'd had? Even if he'd meant everything he'd said, how could their relationship continue with him over here and her back in England?

Reaching the Casino Hospital at ten o'clock that morning, Poppy found a typed message lying on her bed:

> *VAD PEARSON. Please report to Matron's office immediately when you arrive back at the hospital and before going on duty.*

As she washed and changed into a clean uniform, Poppy read the note three or four times over, trying to judge whether Matron was annoyed with her – and, if so, what her defence should be. VADs had to obey so many rules and she hadn't come straight back as she should have done, but when Matron heard that the field doctor had needed Poppy's help with the man on the stretcher, surely she'd understand? As for missing the train – well, with the big offensive on, everyone knew that the trains couldn't be relied on.

Poppy sorted all this out in her head ready to give the correct answers, but when she went into Matron's office, she found, to her horror, that Matron was sitting there taking tea with none other than her old opponent, Sister Sherwood. There had been rumours that this lady, now completely recovered from her septic hand, was returning to the hospital, but Poppy had been trying to ignore them.

Poppy said good morning to them both and managed to smile, but when they stared at her rather coldly, the smile died on her face. She wasn't asked to sit down, even though there was a spare chair in the room.

'You've come back, then, Pearson?' Matron said drily. 'You've been away so long, I rather thought you'd gone Absent Without Leave.'

'Certainly not, Matron. It's just that the trains were very unreliable.'

Two pairs of eyes looked at her keenly.

'And how did your task go?' Matron asked.

Poppy hesitated. They would already know that Patient X had died before she and Michael had got there, but how much else did they know? How much did they need to know? 'As I'm sure you will have heard, the patient died,' she said. 'We were . . . I was . . . terribly sorry. I didn't even see him.'

'And what happened after that?' Matron asked. 'Did you come straight back to the hospital as you were instructed? As you know, your paperwork only gave you permission to be away for one particular and important job.'

Poppy could feel colour coming to her cheeks. 'We were about to leave, Matron, when I was asked to do something by one of the clearing station doctors.'

'Do you always do what doctors ask you?' Sister Sherwood put in.

Poppy said yes, then, fearing that must be a trick question, changed it to no.

'Then what happened?' Matron asked.

'After that, knowing we – that is, Doctor Archer and I – had missed our train, we walked towards the sidings hoping to pick up another.'

'And?'

'And . . .' Poppy hesitated and thought of the way she'd tripped up, how she'd fallen into his arms, the way they'd kissed . . .

'Well?' Sister Sherwood asked sharply.

'The train we'd hoped to get never arrived, and we didn't manage to catch one back to Boulogne until early this morning.'

'And that was all that happened, was it?' Sister Sherwood asked. She looked over her spectacles at Matron. 'As I said, when I was in charge of Ward 5, I'm afraid I had cause to speak severely to this young woman on several occasions.' Her voice dropped. 'She made a habit of being overfamiliar with the patients even then.'

'I certainly did not!' Poppy said hotly.

'No?' said Sister. 'And I suppose you'll deny, too, that it was you asleep in the bunker at the sidings in Albert last night, sprawled on some sacks with a man like . . . like a common prostitute?'

Poppy gasped. That was why Sister Shrew was here – she'd been on that train, seen her and come to report her to Matron.

'Yes, miss, you may well gasp,' said Sister. 'And if I saw you, how many others did? You were visible, bold as brass, to everyone on that train who cared to glance from the window.'

'Is this true, Pearson?' Matron asked.

Poppy felt anger burning inside her. 'I was not sprawled!' she said fiercely. 'I beg your pardon, Matron, but I couldn't help it if I fell asleep. It had been a very long and upsetting day.'

'Such lax morals!' Sister Sherwood snapped. 'Girls like you bring the whole nursing profession into disrepute.'

'You are well aware of the rules, Pearson,' Matron said. 'You know how important it is that British nurses behave with decorum, especially when they are abroad and representing their country.'

'You stayed out overnight with a man,' interrupted Sister Sherwood in an icy, precise tone. 'What on earth will those who saw you from the train be thinking about the nursing profession now?'

Poppy bit her lip to stop herself from crying. She wanted to stamp her foot, thump on the table, demand that they see how unfair they were being, but she feared the consequences if she did such things.

'I'm afraid this young woman is beyond redemption,' said Sister.

Matron nodded. 'Occasionally we do have trouble with VADs and a girl is sent back to England in disgrace,' she said, while Sister Sherwood sat there, a look of satisfaction on her face. 'In these cases I usually allow a girl to work until the end of the month, but your behaviour has been so wanton, your morals so low, that I'm afraid you must receive a dishonourable discharge and leave the hospital – and France – immediately.'

'No!' Poppy gasped.

'Matron has already seen Sister Gradley and acquainted her with the situation,' said Sister Sherwood. She nodded sagely at Matron. 'Lack of moral fibre is contagious. It spreads among the young like a rash.'

They began to discuss which ship Poppy should go home on, while she stood in a fog of dismay, utterly horrified. Choosing to go home and care for her sick mother was one thing, but a dishonourable discharge quite another. With that on her record, she knew she'd never be allowed to nurse again.

Just then, outside the office, Poppy could hear a man speaking to Matron's clerk. A moment later, Michael Archer was shown into the room.

'I'm so sorry, Matron,' the clerk said, 'but Doctor Archer insists he has something urgent to say to you.'

Poppy, her throat aching with unshed tears, didn't look in Michael's direction. Why had he come? She couldn't bear the thought of being humiliated in front of him.

'Your appearance is quite irregular, Doctor Archer,' Matron said, looking taken aback. 'The VADs in this hospital are under my care and control.'

'Of course, of course,' Michael Archer agreed. 'But after speaking to Sister Gradley and discovering that

Miss Pearson was in some kind of trouble, I felt I ought to come and say a word or two in her defence.'

Matron pursed her lips. 'I'm afraid Pearson has behaved quite disgracefully by staying out with you overnight,' she said. 'The rules regarding the behaviour of doctors are quite different from the rules for VADs. Even so, I'm surprised that you behaved so irresponsibly. This girl's reputation is ruined.'

'She is dismissed forthwith and will not be permitted to work in any part of the medical service ever again, home or abroad,' said Sister Sherwood.

'But that's just not fair!' Poppy cried.

'It may not be fair, but it's what happens when a VAD decides to spend the night with a total stranger,' came the retort from Sister.

'But we're not strangers!' said Michael.

The three women in the room turned to stare at him.

'Miss Pearson and I were at Netley together and . . .' he reached over and took Poppy's hand, 'I've come to inform you that our relationship is an honest and proper one. We love each other and are engaged to be married. I apologise very sincerely for not being able to get her back here last night, but in view of the circumstances I hope you'll forgive us.'

There was a stunned silence and Poppy gave him a small smile. She was absolutely amazed at what he'd said – quite flabbergasted – but knew how important it was that she shouldn't look as if she was.

'Is this true, Pearson?' Matron asked.

Poppy nodded, her mind whirling. 'I . . . I didn't know how to tell you, or even whether Doctor Archer would want me to.'

'It's perfectly true,' Michael said. 'We intend to marry on our next leave. We know that wives aren't allowed to serve abroad if their husbands are already doing so, and after the wedding Miss Pearson will stay in England.'

'Or perhaps Wales,' Poppy said. 'My mother is unwell and at present living there with my aunt,' she added in reply to Matron's enquiring look.

'I do hope you'll agree that, apart from this misdemeanour – which I must take some of the responsibility for – Miss Pearson is a loyal and hard-working VAD,' Michael said.

Matron nodded slightly.

'And I also hope that you wouldn't attempt to end her nursing career by appending the words "dishonourable discharge" to her name. In my opinion, Miss Pearson is a born nurse.'

There was a moment's silence, then Matron looked at Sister Sherwood.

'I think what we've just heard puts a different complexion on things,' Matron said.

'Perhaps,' said Sister Sherwood rather grudgingly. 'That is, if you're quite happy about one of your nurses staying out overnight with a young man.'

'I would never normally allow such a thing,' Matron said. 'However, if that young man is that nurse's fiancé then . . .' she spread her hands, 'in certain circumstances it might be forgiven. In view of this, and the excellent report of Pearson's work given by Sister Gradley, I think she should be able to leave the Voluntary Aid Detachment on good terms.'

Michael proffered his hand to Matron, then Sister. 'Then thank you both for your understanding,' he said. 'And may I apologise for robbing you of someone who, I'm sure, is one of your best and most capable nurses.'

Poppy and Michael left Matron's office together and walked to the top of the stairs. Here they stopped and stared at each other in a bemused way.

'I feel quite delirious,' Poppy said. 'Delirious or hysterical, I'm not sure which. Did you really just tell them that we're *engaged*?'

He frowned. 'I don't believe so . . .'

Poppy's face paled. 'You did!'

He laughed. 'Of course I did, darling Pearson. I told them that we love each other and that we're about to get married. Do you mind?'

'Do I mind having to marry you?' Poppy closed her eyes for a moment with the sheer thrill of it. 'No, I don't think I mind at all . . .'

Chapter Twenty-Six

P oppy sat on the edge of her bed in the nurses' quarters, trying to make sense of things. It was humid and stuffy down in the basement, but she was shivering. Whether this was with fright, with shock, or because she was sitting there wearing only her thin cotton petticoat, she didn't know.

Beside her on the bed were the small suitcase borrowed from her mother, some movie magazines, the medical dictionary in which she'd kept the cutting about Freddie de Vere, and her bag of washing things. Also on the bed, in a tidy pile ready to be collected, were her two blue VAD dresses, three starched white aprons bearing red crosses and her outdoor uniform. She was sailing home on the *Blue Yonder* on the four o'clock tide.

Two hours had gone by since her interview with Matron and during this time she'd stripped her bed, cleared out her chest of drawers, and written a letter to

Sister Gradley thanking her for her good report and saying how much she'd enjoyed working in Ward 5. She'd added a PS: *I think it would be too upsetting to say goodbye to the boys, so would you kindly give them my love and say I'll miss them very much.*

Following that, she'd written a note to Dot and Tilly: *I'm downstairs in our quarters. If you can possibly get out for ten minutes at dinner time, there's something I have to tell you!* One of the orderlies had kindly delivered this to the girls' hospital.

As Poppy sat there, her head teeming with thoughts, worries and what-ifs, she heard the two American girls on the stairs.

'What's happened that's so important she has to tell us in the middle of the day?' Dot was asking.

'Search me,' Tilly responded. 'Maybe she's been transferred.'

They found Poppy, still rather overwhelmed by events, sitting quietly on her bed. Both girls stood and stared at her.

'Look at you!' Tilly said. 'Didn't the laundry arrive?'

'You'll cause a sensation if you go on the wards like that!'

'What's happened?' Tilly asked. 'Where are you going that you'll need a different uniform?'

Poppy shook her head slowly. 'Where I'm going, I won't need any uniform at all.'

'What?' both girls exclaimed.

Poppy pressed her lips together hard to stop them trembling, then took a breath. 'This is the happiest and worst day of my life!' she said and burst into tears.

'What's happened?' Dot asked. She sat down beside Poppy and put her arm around her shoulders. 'Pearson!' she said mock sternly. 'Do pull yourself together. You're a British nurse!'

Poppy shook her head. She wasn't – that was just it.

'What on earth's been going on?' Tilly asked. 'Do tell.'

There followed several moments, during which both the American girls patted Poppy on the back, said bracing things and urged her to tell them what the matter was – for goodness' sake, they only had ten minutes!

At last, Poppy gave a mighty sniff and blew her nose. 'Well, you see . . . I stayed out all night last night,' she said, her bottom lip wobbling.

'Wow!' breathed Dot.

'Good going,' said Tilly.

'But I was seen by a sister, who reported me to Matron.'

The smiles dropped from their faces.

'Ah. Not so good,' Tilly said. 'But, if one might ask such a thing, why were you out all night?'

'Yesterday I was sent on a . . . well, a kind of mission,' Poppy said. 'I had to go with a doctor to a clearing station and collect an important casualty.' She looked at them. 'The thing was, the doctor I was assigned to turned out to be Michael Archer.'

'The plot thickens!' said Dot.

'Well, let's hope so,' said her friend, her eyes shining.

'Unfortunately, the casualty died even before we got there,' Poppy continued, 'and then through no fault of our own, Michael and I missed the train, and . . .'

'You don't have to go into detail,' Tilly said.

'No, not if you don't want to,' agreed Dot a bit reluctantly.

'But what I haven't told you is that a little while back, my aunt wrote to say that my ma isn't well and they need me at home, so I knew I'd have to give in my notice and go back to look after her.' She blew her nose. 'But then, when I got back to the hospital this morning, Matron sent for me – and was I for it! She thought Michael and I had only just met, and that my conduct had harmed the reputation of British nurses everywhere. And when she said that, Michael –'

'He was up in front of Matron, too?' Tilly squealed.

Poppy nodded. 'Yes, but not because he was in any trouble. He'd gone in to apologise for keeping me out overnight and . . .' she hesitated and looked at the other two wonderingly, 'and I still can't quite believe it, but he told Matron that we've known each other for some time, and that we're in love and going to be married.'

'Oh!' said Tilly and Dot, looking stunned.

'So you're going to marry that lovely man?' Tilly asked after a moment.

'Of course she is!'

'Did he actually propose?' Tilly asked. 'Oh my, do tell us! Did he get down on one knee? And is it a diamond?'

Poppy hesitated. 'Well, he didn't actually propose . . . He just called me his fiancée.'

There was a pause.

'I suppose that's nearly the same thing,' Tilly said.

'But it would be nice if he'd actually asked for your hand in marriage,' Dot said rather wistfully.

Poppy nodded, her mind whirling. Michael loved her – he'd said he loved her, he'd called her his fiancée – but he hadn't officially proposed marriage.

'But why are you sitting here in your smalls?' Dot asked suddenly.

'Because I have to give my uniform back,' Poppy said. 'The thing is, I've got no clothes to wear on the ship home.'

'Then we must find you something of ours,' said Tilly.

A few minutes later, Poppy was kitted out in one of Tilly's skirts, Dot's woollen jacket and a printed blouse that a girl returning to Blighty had left behind.

Dot looked at her, considering. 'You look a little bit of a dog's dinner . . .'

'But it hardly matters – you've got your man,' said Tilly.

Both girls flung their arms about her.

'We have to go, sweetie,' said Dot.

'Give Doctor Michael Archer our very special love,' said Tilly, 'and tell him we're expecting front seats at the wedding . . .'

Poppy had left the hospital and was heading towards the dockyard when she heard the sound of running footsteps. She turned, immensely relieved, just as Michael caught up with her.

'I didn't think you were going to make it!' she said.

'As if I'd let my best girl go back to Blighty without seeing her off,' Michael said, hugging her.

'*Best* girl?' Poppy asked. 'How many of us are there, then?'

He made a *who knows?* gesture with his hands.

Poppy laughed. 'Will you come over to England soon?'

'As soon as ever I can.'

'And . . . Well, excuse me for being so forward, but Dot and Tilly asked me in what manner you proposed marriage and I had to say that, actually, you hadn't officially proposed to me at all.'

He looked at her, shocked. 'Pearson! Do you doubt me?'

'No, but –'

'Darling Pearson.' He put his hand on his heart. 'I love you more than I can say. Would you do me the great honour of becoming Mrs Archer?'

'Michael . . .' Poppy faltered.

'I'm sorry, I haven't got a . . .' Frowning, he rummaged in his pocket, then said, 'Ah.' He pulled out his fob watch, detached its silver key ring and placed it on the third finger of Poppy's left hand. 'There – will that do until I make it back to Blighty?'

'I believe it will,' said Poppy.

As she put her arm through his, a raggedy cheer was heard and they turned, startled, to see the 'up patients' of Ward 5 had gathered on the hospital balcony and were waving and calling encouragement.

Michael pretended to shake his fist at them. 'At least if you're in Blighty I won't have to share you with a ward full of admirers,' he said.

Poppy, laughing, slipped her arm through his, blew the boys on the balcony a kiss, then walked on towards the docks and towards home.

What Happened Next

P oppy went straight to Aunt Ruby's home in Wales then moved her family, including her aunt, back to live in Mayfield. Her mother was treated for melancholia but, once she was back in her own home, with Poppy looking after her, she improved greatly. She was further cheered when she learned that her daughter was going to marry a doctor.

Mary and Jane just needed a firm hand, and Poppy applied some of the discipline she'd gained through her VAD work to bring them to order. She made sure they learned how to knit and both girls joined their local comforts group.

Once her family was settled, Poppy began a training course to become a qualified nurse, completing this in September 1918, just two months before the war ended. Although there was an end to the fighting at this time, there was not an end to the war casualties and their treatment and care went on. Poppy continued to work in military hospitals for several years.

Seeing no reason to wait, Poppy and Michael Archer were married in Mayfield in September 1916. She wore a white dress with a poppy embroidered at the hem, and Mary and Jane were bridesmaids in blue satin (Tilly and Dot sourced the material from the USA).

Poppy had hoped that Matthews would be her maid of honour, but she couldn't get leave. Dress fabric being so hard to come by in France, and the two girls being about the same size, Poppy sent Matthews her wedding dress to wear when she married Stanley.

Sadly, Second Lieutenant de Vere was included in the *Missing in Action, Believed Killed* list after one of the Somme battles.

Some Notes About The Great War

By 1916, the year in which this book is set, people had realised that the war wasn't going to be over any time soon. Battles were fierce and often ground that was gained after one fight was lost in the next. More men were urgently needed in the British Army and 'call-up' was initially introduced for all unmarried men aged 18 to 41.

The Battle of Verdun began in February of that year and had the dubious distinction of being the longest battle of the war, during which nearly a million German and French soldiers were killed or injured. In May, the Battle of Jutland took place on the sea – the only big clash between the English and German navies. In June, preliminary bombardment by the Allies began for what was going to lead to the greatest loss of life in the whole war: the terrible battle known as the Somme.

The Somme
The Battle of the Somme is remembered especially for its dreadful first day, 1st July 1916. The preparatory bombing, which was supposed to have flattened the barbed wire protecting the German trenches, did not have the desired effect, and nearly 20,000 Allied soldiers died on what was to be the bloodiest day in the history of the British Army. Many recruits in the 'Pals' regiments, who had signed up to fight together, perished together. Tanks were used for the first time, but they made little difference to the outcome. The fighting continued through until autumn, when the ground turned into a quagmire, but the battle was not officially halted until November.

The Great War and the USA
At the start of the war, there was public pressure to keep the USA neutral. However, in 1915 the sinking of the ocean liner the *Lusitania* by a German submarine, with the loss of 125 American lives, went some way to turning the USA against Germany. During the early years of the war, groups of American doctors and nurses volunteered to work in medical units in Europe, though the USA did not officially enter the war until April 1917. In

1918, after a year of preparation and training, the American Expeditionary Force joined the Allies in Europe.

The End of the War

When Poppy went back to England, the war still had over two more weary years to go. Despite the terrible battles at Verdun, the Somme and Jutland, 1916 was to prove as indecisive as the years which had gone before. In 1917 the Canadian Corps took Vimy Ridge and the British attacked Arras, but the French Army sustained over 100,000 casualties and there was mutiny in the ranks on a massive scale. Autumn 1917 saw the appalling Battle of Passchendaele, fought almost entirely in mud, with the continuous driving rain sometimes causing soldiers to drown in mud and filthy water. In 1918 the US army crossed the Atlantic, and this tremendous boost to manpower and morale gave the Allies a decisive advantage over the Germans. The Armistice was signed on 11th November 1918.

The Graves of the War Dead

During the Great War, thousands of men were buried on the battlefield by their comrades, often just where they had fallen. When the war was over, huge efforts were made to locate all these bodies and rebury them in more formal settings. The high numbers of casualties produced a new attitude towards the commemoration of the war dead, and in 1918 it was decided that the bodies of soldiers would not be returned to their own countries and that, to avoid class distinctions, all headstones should be identical. The Commonwealth War Graves Commission now cares for the graves and memorials of the 1.7 million servicemen and women who died in the two world wars.

Acknowledgements

I'd like to thank everyone who helped me discover things about the Great War, all of whom contributed in some way towards the writing of this book.

Some of the incidents in this novel are true and are taken from letters home or diaries of the time. I hope that the relatives of whoever wrote them won't mind me borrowing and giving further life to these stories.

This book, the second one about Poppy, meant me going to France and Belgium several times – always a pleasure, and I was glad to have the excuse. I sailed across the Channel with P&O Ferries (www.poferries.com) on their newest luxury boat, and was helped considerably by Visit Flanders (www.visitflanders.com), who supplied me with maps, guidebooks, tours and details of museums.

Taking a train in France, I found myself sitting next to a chap who, by sheer good fortune, was a World War One buff. I'm so sorry but your name got lost in a sea of yellow stickers, but thank you for answering my questions, and also for the DVD.

In Flanders, I started my research at the marvellous In Flanders Fields Museum (thank you, Annick Vandenbilcke), then visited some of the smaller and more homespun collections. I also visited Talbot House in Poperinge (which is much as it used to be; you can still have bed and breakfast), where Derek and Eira Richards kindly showed me around. Each night I was in Belgium I attended the very moving Last Post ceremony at the Menin Gate, which is held in Ypres at 8.00 p.m. every day.

Dave Goldberg made me a file showing the Great War in one hundred photographs, which has been very useful for school visits. Mike Willoughby has a travelling exhibition about the men of Henley-on-Thames who were involved in the Great War, and knows the answers to the sorts of things you can't find in books.

The Imperial War Museum is much more lively and interesting than its name suggests, but was, unfortunately, closed for redevelopment while I was doing my research.

The internet has been invaluable, and it was Cathy and John Huddy who discovered and told me of the wonderful Scarlet Finders website (www.scarletfinders. co.uk), with everything you could possibly want to know about VADs. The Long, Long Trail website (www.1914-1918.net) was also very helpful.

Lastly, I'd like to say that the Casino Hospital is fictitious, and that any mistakes are entirely my own.

Bibliography

Appleton, Edith, *A Nurse at the Front: The First World War Diaries of Sister Edith Appleton*, Simon and Schuster, 2012

Atkinson, Diane, *Elsie and Mairi Go to War: Two Extraordinary Women on the Western Front*, Arrow, 2010

Bagnold, Enid, *A Diary Without Dates*, Virago, 1978

Brittain, Vera, *Testament of Youth*, Virago, 1978

Cohen, Susan, *Medical Services in the First World War*, Shire Publications, 2014

Hill, Duncan, *The Great War – A Pictorial History*, Atlantic Publishing, 2013

MacDonald, Lyn, *The Roses of No Man's Land*, Penguin, 1993

Powell, Anne, *Women in the War Zone – Hospital Service in the First World War*, The History Press, 2009

Rathbone, Irene, *We That Were Young*, Virago, 1988

Robertshaw, Andrew, *Somme – 1 July 1916*, Osprey Publishing, 2006

Storey, Neil R. and Housego, Molly, *Women in the First World War*, Shire Publications, 2011

'Mary Hooper is one of our finest writers of historical romance'
Amanda Craig, The Times

ENGLAND, DECEMBER 1914

Poppy is young, beautiful and clever – and working as a parlourmaid
in the de Vere family's country house. Society, it seems, has already
carved out her destiny.

But Poppy's life is about to be thrown dramatically off course. The
first reason is love – with someone forbidden, who could never, ever
marry a girl like her. The second reason is war.

As the lists of the dead and wounded grow longer, Poppy must do
whatever she can to help the injured soldiers, knowing all the while
that her own soldier may never return home . . .

A sweeping, romantic, heartbreaking novel set against the backdrop of
World War I

www.maryhooper.co.uk

'Another sumptuous, satisfying read from Mary Hooper'
Lucy Mangan

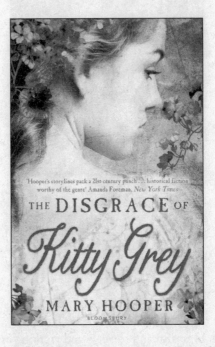

'Hooper's storylines pack a 21st-century punch . . . historical fiction
worthy of the genre' Amanda Foreman, *New York Times*

THE DISGRACE OF

Kitty Grey

MARY HOOPER

BLOOMSBURY

Kitty has a comfortable life as a country milkmaid. She is well
looked after by the family who live up at the great house, and she
enjoys being courted by Will Villiers, the handsome river man.
Then, one day, Will vanishes.

Kitty is heartbroken, and when sent to London on an errand, she
is determined to track down Will. But, alone and vulnerable in
the vast city, Kitty's fate is snatched out of her hands and she is
plunged into a dizzying spiral of despair . . .

A thrilling tale of betrayal, love and true courage.

www.maryhooper.co.uk